Table of Con

Chapter 1: The Roots of Terrorism

What is terrorism?

The origins of terrorism are deeply entwined with historical, sociopolitical, and psychological factors that coalesce to create a complex and multifaceted phenomenon. Historically, terrorism can be traced back to ancient times, where it was employed as a tool of political coercion and intimidation. The Zealots of Judea, for instance, used tactics that would be considered terrorism today to resist Roman occupation. The concept of terrorism as a structured practice, however, began to crystallize in the late 18th century with the French Revolution's Reign of Terror, where state-sponsored violence was used to eliminate opposition and instill fear among the populace. This period marked a significant shift, illustrating how terrorism could be wielded by both state and non-state actors to achieve political ends.

Sociopolitically, terrorism often emerges from environments characterized by instability, oppression, and social injustice. Marginalized groups, feeling disenfranchised and powerless, may turn to terrorism as a means to challenge the status quo and assert their demands. The colonial and post-colonial eras provide numerous examples of this dynamic, where nationalist movements resorted to terrorist tactics to expel foreign occupiers and establish independent states. The Irish Republican Army (IRA) and the Palestine Liberation Organization (PLO) are notable examples, illustrating how nationalist aspirations and resistance against perceived imperialist forces can drive groups towards terrorism.

Psychologically, the motivations behind terrorism are equally complex. Individuals involved in terrorist activities often exhibit a blend of ideological fervor, personal grievances, and a desire for social belonging. The concept of "collective identity" plays a crucial role, as terrorist organizations provide a sense of purpose and community to individuals who may feel alienated from mainstream society. This sense of belonging is reinforced through shared ideologies and narratives that justify violence as a legitimate means to achieve their goals. The radicalization process, which transforms individuals into terrorists, often involves a combination of personal experiences, exposure to extremist ideologies, and social networks that facilitate the adoption of violent behaviors.

The role of ideology in terrorism cannot be overstated. Ideologies serve as the glue that binds terrorist organizations together, providing a framework for understanding the world and legitimizing violent actions. Religious, nationalist, and revolutionary ideologies are among the most common, each offering a distinct narrative that rationalizes terrorism as a necessary and justifiable response to perceived injustices. Religious terrorism, in particular, has gained prominence in recent decades, with groups like Al-Qaeda and ISIS using religious narratives to recruit and motivate members. These ideologies often portray the world in stark, binary terms, casting the terrorists as defenders of a righteous cause against an evil adversary.

State sponsorship of terrorism adds another layer of complexity. States may support terrorist groups to advance their geopolitical interests, exert influence in a region, or destabilize rival governments. This support can take various forms, including funding, training, and providing safe havens. The relationship between state sponsors and terrorist groups is often symbiotic, with both parties benefiting from the arrangement. However, this dynamic also complicates efforts to combat terrorism, as it blurs the lines between state and non-state actors and complicates international legal frameworks.

The impact of globalization on terrorism is profound. Advances in technology and communication have enabled terrorist groups to expand their reach, recruit members globally, and disseminate propaganda more effectively. The internet and social media, in particular, have transformed the landscape of terrorism, allowing groups to radicalize and mobilize individuals across vast distances. This digital revolution has also facilitated the spread of extremist ideologies and the coordination of attacks, making it increasingly challenging for authorities to counteract these threats.

Economic factors also play a significant role in the rise of terrorism. Poverty, lack of education, and economic inequality can create fertile ground for terrorist recruitment. Individuals in economically deprived regions may find the promise of financial reward or the prospect of social mobility through terrorist organizations appealing. terrorist groups often exploit economic grievances to garner support, framing their struggle as a fight against economic exploitation and inequality.

The psychological profiles of terrorists reveal a diverse range of motivations and characteristics. Contrary to popular belief, not all terrorists are driven by mental illness or pathological conditions. Many are rational actors who make calculated decisions based on their ideological convictions and strategic goals. However, certain psychological traits, such as a propensity for violence, a lack of empathy, and a willingness to engage in high-risk behaviors, are more prevalent among terrorists. The process of radicalization often involves a gradual shift in beliefs and attitudes, influenced by personal experiences and social interactions.

Understanding the social networks within terrorist organizations is crucial for comprehending how they operate and sustain themselves. These networks provide the social capital that enables terrorist groups to function effectively, offering logistical support, intelligence, and a sense of community. The structure of these networks can vary, with some groups organized in hierarchical, centralized formations, while others operate in decentralized, cell-based structures. The latter has become increasingly common, as it provides greater resilience against law enforcement and intelligence agencies.

The role of charismatic leaders in terrorist organizations cannot be overlooked. Leaders like Osama bin Laden and Abu Bakr al-Baghdadi have been instrumental in shaping the direction and strategies of their respective organizations. These leaders often possess a compelling vision, strong rhetorical skills, and the ability to inspire loyalty and commitment among their followers. Their influence extends beyond operational decision-making, shaping the ideological and strategic foundations of the group.

The impact of state policies on the proliferation of terrorism is a critical area of study. Repressive policies, human rights abuses, and political exclusion can exacerbate the conditions that give rise to terrorism. Conversely, policies that promote inclusivity, economic development, and political participation can mitigate these conditions. The challenge for policymakers is to strike a balance between security measures and respect for civil liberties, ensuring that counterterrorism efforts do not inadvertently fuel the very phenomenon they seek to eradicate.

The relationship between terrorism and the media is a double-edged sword. On one hand, media coverage can amplify the impact of terrorist attacks, spreading fear and anxiety among the public. On the other hand, media can play a crucial role in countering terrorist narratives and promoting awareness and understanding of the underlying issues driving terrorism. The challenge lies in finding a balance between informing the public and avoiding sensationalism that can further the terrorists' objectives.

Efforts to combat terrorism have evolved over time, with a growing emphasis on international cooperation, intelligence sharing, and addressing the root causes of radicalization. Military interventions, while sometimes necessary, are increasingly recognized as insufficient on their own. Long-term solutions require a comprehensive approach that includes economic development, political reform, and social initiatives aimed at addressing the grievances that fuel terrorism. This holistic approach recognizes that terrorism is not merely a security issue but a complex social phenomenon that demands multifaceted responses. Understanding these roots requires a nuanced approach that considers the diverse motivations and contexts in which terrorism emerges. By addressing the underlying causes and adopting comprehensive strategies, it is possible to mitigate the threat posed by terrorism and promote a more stable and secure world. This analytical exploration of the origins and dynamics of terrorism provides a foundational understanding necessary for developing effective counterterrorism policies and fostering a more informed and empathetic public discourse.

The history of terrorism

The origins of terrorism can be traced back to ancient and medieval times, where various forms of politically motivated violence were practiced. During the Roman Empire, for instance, the Sicarii, a group of Jewish zealots, employed assassination and sabotage to resist Roman rule. Their actions, aimed at destabilizing the occupying forces, are considered early examples of terrorism. In the Middle Ages, the Hashshashins, a sect of Shia Muslims, used targeted assassinations to further their political and religious goals. These historical instances illustrate that terrorism has long been a tool for those seeking to challenge established authorities or achieve specific political outcomes.

The French Revolution marked a significant turning point in the history of terrorism. The period of the Reign of Terror, from 1793 to 1794, introduced state-sponsored terrorism as a means of controlling and suppressing opposition. The Jacobins, led by Maximilien Robespierre, utilized mass executions, public trials, and widespread fear to maintain their grip on power. This period demonstrated the potential of terror as a tool of the state, setting a precedent for future regimes that would employ similar tactics to consolidate their authority.

In the late 19th and early 20th centuries, terrorism began to take on a more modern form, characterized by the rise of anarchism and revolutionary movements. The concept of "propaganda by the deed," promoted by anarchists, emphasized the use of violent acts to inspire revolutionary change. Notable incidents from this era include the assassination of Tsar Alexander II of Russia in 1881 by members of the Narodnaya Volya (People's Will) and the assassination of Archduke Franz Ferdinand of Austria in 1914 by Gavrilo Princip, a member of the Black Hand, which precipitated World War I. These events underscored the impact that targeted acts of violence could have on global politics and the course of history.

The post-World War I era saw the emergence of new forms of terrorism, driven by nationalist and anti-colonial sentiments. In Ireland, the Irish Republican Army (IRA) waged a campaign against British rule, employing tactics such as bombings and assassinations. Similarly, in the Middle East, groups like the Jewish paramilitary organizations Irgun and Lehi used violence to advance their goals of establishing a Jewish state. These movements highlighted the role of terrorism in anti-colonial struggles, demonstrating its effectiveness in drawing attention to the cause and undermining colonial authority.

The latter half of the 20th century witnessed the rise of left-wing and right-wing terrorism, reflecting the ideological conflicts of the Cold War period. Left-wing terrorist groups, such as the Red Army Faction in Germany and the Red Brigades in Italy, sought to overthrow capitalist systems and establish communist states. Their activities included bombings, kidnappings, and assassinations, aimed at destabilizing governments and provoking revolutionary change. On the other hand, right-wing terrorism, exemplified by groups like the Ku Klux Klan in the United States and neo-Nazi organizations in Europe, aimed to preserve or restore hierarchical social orders and combat perceived threats from minority groups. These ideological conflicts underscored the diverse motivations behind terrorist acts and the different strategies employed by various groups.

Religiously motivated terrorism emerged as a significant force in the late 20th and early 21st centuries. This form of terrorism is characterized by its focus on achieving religiously inspired political goals and its willingness to employ extreme violence to attain them. Groups such as Al-Qaeda and later the Islamic State (ISIS) exemplify this trend, using acts of terrorism to challenge Western influence in Muslim-majority countries and to establish Islamic states governed by their interpretation of Sharia law. The September 11, 2001, attacks on the United States by Al-Qaeda, which resulted in the deaths of nearly 3,000 people, marked a watershed moment in the history of terrorism, highlighting the global reach and devastating impact of religiously motivated terrorist groups.

The development of modern terrorism has also been influenced by technological advancements and globalization. The advent of the internet and social media has provided terrorist groups with new platforms for recruitment, propaganda, and coordination. These technologies have enabled groups to reach a wider audience, disseminate their messages more effectively, and inspire lone-wolf attacks by individuals who may have no direct affiliation with the group. Additionally, globalization has facilitated the movement of people, money, and weapons across borders, making it easier for terrorist organizations to operate on an international scale.

Understanding the historical roots of terrorism requires an examination of the socio-political contexts in which it arises. Economic deprivation, political oppression, and social alienation are often cited as factors that contribute to the emergence of terrorist movements. In many cases, terrorist groups exploit these conditions to recruit members and garner support for their cause. The perception of injustice and the desire for revenge or recognition also play significant roles in motivating individuals to engage in terrorist activities.

The psychological dimension of terrorism is another critical aspect that must be considered. The process of radicalization, whereby individuals come to embrace extremist ideologies and are willing to use violence to achieve their goals, involves a complex interplay of personal, social, and ideological factors. Research has shown that there is no single profile of a terrorist, and the pathways to radicalization can vary widely. Factors such as personal grievances, group dynamics, and the influence of charismatic leaders can all contribute to the process of radicalization. From ancient assassins to modern jihadists, terrorists have employed a range of tactics and strategies to achieve their objectives. Understanding this history is essential for developing effective counterterrorism strategies and addressing the root causes of terrorism. By examining the past, we can gain valuable insights into the motivations and methods of terrorist groups, enabling us to better anticipate and respond to the challenges posed by terrorism in the contemporary world.

Motivations for terrorism

One of the primary motivations for terrorism is the pursuit of political power and change. Terrorist groups often emerge in environments where legitimate political channels are perceived as ineffective or inaccessible. In such contexts, violence is seen as a means to challenge the status quo, garner attention, and force concessions from the state or other authorities. Historical examples, such as the Irish Republican Army (IRA) or the Basque separatist group ETA, illustrate how nationalist and separatist aspirations can drive terrorist activities. These groups resort to violence as a tool to achieve political autonomy or independence, reflecting a deep-seated belief that peaceful or democratic means are insufficient to address their grievances.

Ideological motivations also play a crucial role in the emergence of terrorism. Ideologies, whether religious, political, or social, provide a framework that justifies and legitimizes the use of violence. Religious extremism, in particular, has been a significant driver of terrorism in recent decades. Groups such as Al-Qaeda and ISIS draw on radical interpretations of Islamic teachings to justify their actions, portraying violence as a divine duty. This religiously inspired terrorism often aims to establish a theocratic state or to defend a perceived Islamic community from external threats. The ideological fervor associated with such beliefs can create a powerful incentive for individuals to engage in terrorist activities, as they view their actions as part of a broader, sacred mission.

Socioeconomic factors also contribute significantly to the motivations behind terrorism. In many cases, terrorists come from backgrounds characterized by poverty, lack of education, and limited economic opportunities. These conditions can create a sense of hopelessness and marginalization, making individuals more susceptible to recruitment by terrorist organizations. The promise of financial rewards, social status, or a sense of belonging can be powerful motivators, especially in regions where economic disparities and social injustices are rampant. terrorist groups often exploit these conditions to recruit and indoctrinate vulnerable individuals, offering them a sense of purpose and a way to express their frustrations and grievances.

Psychological motivations for terrorism, though less tangible, are equally important. Individuals involved in terrorism often exhibit certain psychological traits, such as a propensity for risk-taking, a desire for significance, and a need for identity and belonging. The act of terrorism can provide a sense of empowerment and control to individuals who feel powerless in their everyday lives. Additionally, the dynamics of group psychology, such as peer pressure and the need for acceptance, can influence individuals to adopt extremist views and engage in violent actions. The process of radicalization often involves a combination of personal grievances and exposure to extremist ideologies, which collectively contribute to the psychological readiness to commit acts of terrorism.

Another critical motivation for terrorism is the desire for revenge and retaliation. Acts of terrorism are often responses to perceived injustices or aggressions, whether real or imagined. This retributive aspect can be seen in various contexts, including responses to military interventions, foreign policies, or domestic policies that are viewed as oppressive or discriminatory. For instance, terrorist attacks in retaliation for Western military interventions in the Middle East exemplify how grievances over foreign occupation or perceived imperialism can drive terrorist activities. The cycle of violence and retaliation can create a self-perpetuating dynamic, where each act of terrorism begets further violence, perpetuating a seemingly endless cycle of conflict.

Terrorism can also be motivated by a desire to provoke a reaction from the state or international community. Terrorist acts are sometimes designed to elicit an overreaction from governments, which can lead to repression, human rights abuses, and increased public support for the terrorists' cause. This strategy, often referred to as "propaganda of the deed," aims to expose the perceived brutality and illegitimacy of the state, thereby undermining its authority and legitimacy. The hope is that such reactions will radicalize more individuals and swell the ranks of the terrorist movement, creating a broader base of support and complicating the state's efforts to combat the threat effectively.

Cultural and identity-based motivations cannot be overlooked when examining the roots of terrorism. In many cases, terrorist movements are driven by a desire to preserve or promote a particular cultural or ethnic identity in the face of perceived threats. This can be particularly relevant in regions with diverse populations or where cultural identities are closely tied to political aspirations. The rise of ethno-nationalist terrorism, as seen in conflicts in the Balkans or parts of Africa, highlights how cultural and ethnic identities can become powerful motivators for violence. The struggle to maintain or assert cultural dominance can lead to extreme measures, including terrorist acts, as groups seek to defend their heritage and way of life.

The role of charismatic leadership in motivating terrorism is also significant. Leaders of terrorist organizations often possess a charismatic appeal that can inspire and mobilize followers. These leaders use their influence to articulate a compelling vision, justify the use of violence, and provide a sense of direction and purpose. The personal charisma of leaders like Osama bin Laden or Abdullah Öcalan has played a crucial role in the growth and sustainment of terrorist movements. Charismatic leaders can create a cult-like following, where followers are willing to commit acts of violence out of loyalty and devotion to their leader and the cause they represent.

In ending, technological advancements and the globalization of communication have introduced new motivations and opportunities for terrorism. The internet and social media provide platforms for the dissemination of extremist ideologies, recruitment, and coordination of terrorist activities. Cyber-terrorism, for example, leverages technology to disrupt critical infrastructure and spread fear. Additionally, the global reach of the internet allows terrorist groups to transcend geographical boundaries, recruit members from diverse backgrounds, and inspire lone-wolf attacks. The anonymity and accessibility of online platforms make it easier for individuals to become radicalized and engage in terrorism, often without direct physical contact with a terrorist organization. Understanding these motivations requires a comprehensive and interdisciplinary approach that considers the diverse contexts in which terrorism arises. By examining the interplay of these factors, we can gain deeper insights into the

roots of terrorism and develop more effective strategies to address
and mitigate this persistent global challenge.

Chapter 2: The Psychology of Terrorists

The personality traits of terrorists

Another critical trait is the propensity for aggression. While not all aggressive individuals become terrorists, a heightened predisposition towards aggression can be a common denominator among those who do. This aggression can stem from a variety of sources, including past experiences of violence or trauma, social conditioning, or ideological indoctrination. Importantly, this aggression is often channeled through a framework that justifies violent actions against perceived enemies, thus providing a moral and ideological rationale for their behavior.

A notable characteristic among many terrorists is a lack of empathy. This diminished capacity for empathy allows individuals to commit acts of violence without the emotional distress that typically accompanies such actions. This emotional detachment is crucial for carrying out terrorist activities, as it enables individuals to dehumanize their victims and view them as legitimate targets. The process of radicalization often involves a systematic devaluation of the 'other,' which further erodes empathetic responses and facilitates violent behavior.

The role of identity and group dynamics cannot be overstated in understanding terrorist psychology. Many terrorists exhibit a strong identification with a particular group or cause, which serves to reinforce their beliefs and actions. This group identity provides a sense of belonging and purpose, which can be particularly compelling for individuals who feel alienated from mainstream society. Within these groups, a sense of camaraderie and shared purpose often overrides individual moral qualms, leading to a collective rationalization of violence.

terrorists often display a pronounced sense of grievance. This grievance can be rooted in real or perceived injustices, which are frequently amplified by ideological narratives. The sense of grievance acts as a powerful motivator, driving individuals to seek retribution and justice through violent means. This sense of mission can be so compelling that it overrides conventional moral and ethical considerations, justifying extreme actions in the minds of the perpetrators.

Cognitive rigidity is another trait frequently observed in terrorists. This inflexibility in thinking manifests as an inability to entertain alternative viewpoints or to engage in critical self-reflection. Cognitive rigidity often results from exposure to extremist propaganda, which presents a narrow, black-and-white worldview. This rigidity reinforces a sense of certainty and righteousness, making individuals more susceptible to radicalization and less likely to reconsider their actions or beliefs.

Terrorists also tend to exhibit a high degree of risk-taking behavior. This propensity for risk is often linked to a desire for notoriety and a willingness to engage in actions that most people would find unacceptable. The thrill-seeking aspect of terrorism can be particularly appealing to younger individuals, who may be drawn to the excitement and drama of extremist activities. This risk-taking behavior is further amplified by the ideological conviction that their cause is justified, making them more willing to undertake dangerous missions.

The role of ideology in shaping terrorist behavior is paramount. Ideology provides a framework that justifies and legitimizes violence, offering a sense of purpose and direction. For many terrorists, ideological beliefs are central to their identity and actions. These beliefs are often deeply ingrained and resistant to change, as they provide a lens through which individuals interpret their experiences and justify their actions. The power of ideology lies in its ability to transform individual grievances and aggression into a collective, morally justified struggle.

Social and environmental factors play a crucial role in shaping terrorist personalities. Individuals from marginalized communities or those experiencing social upheaval are more susceptible to radicalization. The experience of social exclusion, discrimination, or political oppression can foster a sense of alienation and resentment, making extremist ideologies more attractive. These social factors interact with personal traits, creating a fertile ground for the emergence of terrorist tendencies.

Furthermore, the process of radicalization often involves a convergence of personal and contextual factors. Personal vulnerabilities, such as a history of trauma, psychological distress, or social isolation, can intersect with broader contextual factors, such as political instability or exposure to extremist propaganda. This convergence creates a pathway to radicalization, where individuals are gradually drawn into extremist networks and ideologies. The role of social networks, both online and offline, is critical in this process, as they provide the social support and reinforcement necessary for radicalization.

The psychological concept of moral disengagement is also central to understanding terrorist behavior. Moral disengagement refers to the cognitive processes that allow individuals to engage in unethical behavior without feeling guilt or shame. For terrorists, moral disengagement involves justifying violence through ideological narratives that frame their actions as necessary and righteous. This cognitive restructuring allows individuals to override conventional moral inhibitions, facilitating the commission of acts of terror.

In addition to these traits, the concept of 'instrumental aggression' is pertinent. Instrumental aggression is aggression that is used as a means to an end, rather than as an expression of anger or frustration. For terrorists, violence is often a strategic tool used to achieve specific political or ideological goals. This instrumental approach to violence underscores the calculated and deliberate nature of terrorist activities, which are often planned and executed with specific objectives in mind.

The role of charismatic leadership in terrorist organizations cannot be overlooked. Charismatic leaders often possess a magnetic personality that attracts and inspires followers. These leaders are adept at articulating a compelling vision and mobilizing individuals around a common cause. Their influence can be profound, shaping the beliefs and actions of their followers and fostering a sense of loyalty and commitment. The presence of a charismatic leader can significantly enhance the cohesion and effectiveness of terrorist groups, making them more dangerous and resilient. Understanding these traits requires a nuanced approach that considers the interplay of individual vulnerabilities, social dynamics, and ideological influences. By examining these factors, we can gain deeper insights into the minds of terrorists and develop more effective strategies for countering radicalization and preventing acts of terror.

The cognitive processes of terrorists

At the core of the terrorist's cognitive process is the adoption of a simplistic, binary worldview. This Manichean perspective divides the world into absolute categories of good and evil, us versus them. Such a dichotomous outlook simplifies the complex socio-political landscape into a straightforward battle between opposing forces. This cognitive simplification allows terrorists to categorize themselves as the righteous combatants fighting against an unjust and malevolent enemy. The psychological comfort derived from this clarity of purpose is significant, as it provides a sense of moral superiority and absolute certainty in their cause.

Dehumanization of the enemy is another crucial cognitive process in the terrorist mindset. By viewing their adversaries as less than human, terrorists can circumvent the natural human aversion to violence. This dehumanization is often achieved through propaganda that portrays the enemy as inherently evil, subhuman, or a threat to the terrorists' way of life. The repeated exposure to such narratives erodes empathy and fosters a sense of detachment, making it psychologically easier for terrorists to commit acts of violence against their perceived enemies.

The internalization of an overarching, often apocalyptic narrative is a powerful cognitive tool in the terrorist's arsenal. This narrative provides a grand, overarching story that imbues their actions with a sense of historical or religious significance. For many terrorists, this narrative is rooted in a belief that their struggle is part of a larger, cosmic battle between good and evil. This belief system can be secular or religious, but it invariably provides a sense of purpose and destiny. The apocalyptic nature of this narrative often leads terrorists to believe that their actions will precipitate a dramatic, transformative event that will usher in a new world order.

Cognitive biases play a significant role in shaping the terrorist mindset. One of the most prevalent biases is confirmation bias, where terrorists selectively seek out and interpret information that confirms their preexisting beliefs while ignoring or dismissing contradictory evidence. This cognitive bias reinforces their conviction and justifies their violent actions by creating an echo chamber of supportive information. Similarly, the availability heuristic, where individuals overestimate the likelihood of events based on their vividness or emotional impact, can lead terrorists to overestimate the threat posed by their enemies or the effectiveness of their violent actions.

The role of group dynamics in shaping terrorist cognition cannot be overstated. Terrorists often operate within tightly knit groups that reinforce their beliefs and behaviors. Groupthink, a phenomenon where the desire for consensus and cohesion within a group leads to irrational or dysfunctional decision-making, is prevalent among terrorist organizations. The intense pressure to conform within these groups can suppress dissenting opinions and lead to a further entrenchment of extremist views. Additionally, the sense of camaraderie and belonging provided by these groups can be a powerful motivator, as individuals derive a strong sense of identity and purpose from their membership.

The concept of moral disengagement is crucial in understanding how terrorists reconcile their violent actions with their moral and ethical beliefs. Moral disengagement involves a set of cognitive mechanisms that allow individuals to disengage their moral self-sanctions, thereby enabling them to commit acts they would otherwise deem reprehensible. Techniques such as euphemistic labeling, advantageous comparison, and displacement of responsibility are commonly employed by terrorists. Euphemistic labeling involves using sanitized or euphemistic terms to describe violent actions, such as referring to terrorism as "resistance" or "liberation. " Advantageous comparison involves comparing their actions to those of their enemies, thereby justifying their violence as a necessary response to the perceived greater evil of their adversaries. Displacement of responsibility shifts the blame for their actions onto authority figures or the group, thereby absolving individuals of personal guilt.

The cognitive process of radicalization is a gradual and often complex journey that involves a series of cognitive shifts. Initially, individuals may be exposed to extremist ideologies through various channels, such as social media, peer networks, or charismatic leaders. Over time, these ideas are reinforced through repeated exposure and social reinforcement within like-minded groups. The process of radicalization involves a deepening commitment to the extremist ideology and an increasing willingness to engage in violent action. This radicalization process is often facilitated by cognitive opening, where individuals are in a state of psychological vulnerability or transition, making them more susceptible to extremist ideologies.

Terrorists often employ a form of cognitive restructuring to prepare themselves for violent action. This process involves a systematic alteration of their beliefs, attitudes, and behaviors to align with the demands of their extremist ideology. Cognitive restructuring can include desensitization to violence, training in combat and weaponry, and psychological conditioning to overcome fear and doubt. The terrorist's cognitive framework is thus reshaped to accommodate the requirements of their violent mission, making them more effective and committed operatives.

The role of emotion in terrorist cognition is also significant. While the popular perception of terrorists is often one of cold, calculating individuals, emotions such as anger, hatred, and a desire for revenge play a crucial role in their cognitive processes. These emotions can act as powerful motivators, driving individuals to commit acts of violence in response to perceived injustices or personal grievances. The emotional intensity of these experiences can override rational thought processes, leading to impulsive and extreme actions.

Another cognitive process that is central to the terrorist mindset is the construction of a martyrdom narrative. Many terrorists view their violent actions as a form of sacrificial act that will grant them a revered status within their ideological community. This martyrdom narrative provides a powerful incentive for individuals to engage in acts of terrorism, as they believe that their death will be memorialized and celebrated. The promise of eternal reward, whether in a secular or religious context, can be a potent motivator, making the ultimate sacrifice seem not only justified but also desirable.

The cognitive processes of terrorists are also influenced by their perceptions of legitimacy and injustice. Many terrorists believe that their actions are a legitimate response to what they perceive as unjust conditions or oppressive regimes. This perception of injustice is often magnified and distorted through the lens of their extremist ideology, leading them to view their violence as a necessary and justifiable means of achieving their goals. This sense of moral righteousness further entrenches their commitment to violence and can make them impervious to efforts at negotiation or reconciliation.

The concept of identity fusion is another important cognitive process in the terrorist mindset. Identity fusion occurs when an individual's personal identity becomes deeply intertwined with their group identity. This intense sense of unity and shared purpose can lead to an unwavering commitment to the group's cause and a willingness to engage in extreme acts of violence on its behalf. The fused identity provides a powerful source of motivation and resilience, as individuals derive a profound sense of meaning and belonging from their group membership. Understanding these cognitive processes is crucial for developing effective strategies to counter terrorism, as it allows for a deeper insight into the psychological mechanisms that drive individuals to commit acts of violence. By addressing the underlying cognitive factors that contribute to terrorism, it is possible to develop more nuanced and effective approaches to prevention and intervention.

The emotional experiences of terrorists

One prominent emotional experience among terrorists is a profound sense of anger and resentment. This anger often stems from perceived injustices, whether real or imagined, that the individual or their community has endured. These grievances can be political, social, or economic in nature, and they serve as powerful motivators for joining terrorist organizations. For many terrorists, this anger is directed towards governments, institutions, or other groups they view as oppressors. This intense anger can fuel a desire for revenge, which is a potent driving force behind violent actions.

In addition to anger, many terrorists experience a deep sense of alienation and disenfranchisement. This feeling of being disconnected from mainstream society can be a significant factor in radicalization. Individuals who feel marginalized or excluded may seek out groups that offer a sense of belonging and purpose. Terrorist organizations often exploit these feelings, providing a sense of community and identity to individuals who feel they have none. This camaraderie and shared purpose can be emotionally fulfilling, filling a void left by societal exclusion.

Fear is another critical emotion experienced by terrorists, although it is often overshadowed by their outward displays of aggression and defiance. The fear of being caught, the fear of failing in their mission, and the fear of death are all prevalent. However, these fears are frequently managed through ideological indoctrination and group dynamics. Terrorist organizations often use religious or political ideologies to downplay the significance of fear, framing martyrdom or sacrifice as noble and necessary for the cause. This manipulation of fear can transform it into a source of motivation rather than an impediment.

The emotional experience of terrorists also includes a significant degree of moral disengagement. This psychological mechanism allows individuals to commit acts of violence without experiencing the associated guilt or remorse. By dehumanizing their victims and viewing their actions as justified or even righteous, terrorists can dissociate themselves from the moral implications of their behavior. This moral disengagement is facilitated by the group's ideology and the normalization of violence within the terrorist organization.

Furthermore, terrorists often experience a heightened sense of excitement and exhilaration. The act of engaging in violent activities can be thrilling, providing an adrenaline rush that is both addictive and empowering. This excitement can be particularly pronounced in individuals who have lived relatively mundane or oppressed lives. The opportunity to engage in actions that they believe will significantly impact the world can be exhilarating, providing a sense of purpose and significance that was previously lacking.

In contrast to the excitement, terrorists may also experience profound feelings of guilt and inner conflict. Despite the ideological justifications provided by their groups, some individuals struggle with the ethical and moral implications of their actions. This guilt can be particularly intense after acts of violence that result in significant harm or loss of life. The internal conflict between their actions and their moral beliefs can lead to psychological distress, although this is often suppressed or rationalized away through further indoctrination.

The role of grief and loss in the emotional experiences of terrorists should not be overlooked. Many terrorists have experienced personal losses, such as the death of loved ones due to conflict, oppression, or state violence. These experiences of loss can be deeply traumatic and can fuel a desire for retribution. Grief can be a powerful emotion that drives individuals towards radicalization, as they seek to avenge their losses and prevent further suffering.

The emotional bond within terrorist groups is also a critical aspect of their emotional experiences. The sense of brotherhood or sisterhood that develops within these groups can be incredibly strong. This bond is fostered through shared experiences, mutual goals, and the intense emotional experiences of engaging in violent actions together. This camaraderie can provide a powerful emotional support system, reinforcing the individual's commitment to the group and its cause.

The emotional experiences of terrorists are also shaped by their interactions with the broader society. The reactions of the public, media, and government to their actions can influence their emotional states. For example, widespread condemnation and punitive measures can reinforce their sense of alienation and victimhood, strengthening their resolve and commitment to their cause. Conversely, attempts at dialogue and understanding can sometimes mitigate these negative emotions, although this is a complex and delicate process.

The impact of propaganda and indoctrination on the emotional experiences of terrorists cannot be overstated. Terrorist organizations often use sophisticated propaganda techniques to manipulate the emotions of their members. This propaganda can evoke powerful emotions such as anger, fear, and a sense of urgency, driving individuals to commit acts of violence. The constant exposure to extremist ideologies and narratives can shape the emotional landscape of terrorists, making it difficult for them to envision alternative perspectives or solutions.

The emotional experiences of terrorists are also influenced by their interactions with victims and the consequences of their actions. For some, the direct experience of violence and its aftermath can lead to a reassessment of their beliefs and actions. Witnessing the suffering caused by their violence can evoke feelings of guilt, regret, and horror. However, for others, these experiences can further entrench their commitment to violence, as they rationalize the suffering as necessary for their cause.

The emotional toll of engaging in terrorist activities can lead to significant psychological distress. Symptoms of anxiety, depression, and post-traumatic stress disorder (PTSD) are not uncommon among terrorists. The constant threat of capture or death, combined with the psychological burden of their actions, can lead to severe mental health issues. However, these symptoms are often masked or denied due to the stigma associated with mental health issues within many terrorist organizations. Understanding these emotional experiences is crucial for developing effective counterterrorism strategies that address the root causes of radicalization and violence. By acknowledging and addressing the emotional dimensions of terrorism, it is possible to develop more nuanced and effective approaches to preventing and combating terrorist activities.

Chapter 3: The Organizational Structure of Terrorist Groups

The types of terrorist groups

Hierarchical terrorist organizations are characterized by a clear chain of command, with distinct levels of authority and responsibility. This structure resembles that of traditional military or corporate organizations, with a central leadership directing activities and making strategic decisions. The top tier typically consists of the most senior leaders, who are responsible for overall strategy, resource allocation, and major decisions. Beneath them are mid-level commanders who oversee specific regions or functions, such as logistics, recruitment, or operations. The lowest tier includes foot soldiers or operatives who carry out the directives from above. This structure allows for efficient coordination and control but can be vulnerable to decapitation strikes—targeted eliminations of top leaders—which can severely disrupt operations and morale.

One of the most well-known examples of a hierarchical terrorist group is Al-Qaeda. Under the leadership of Osama bin Laden, Al-Qaeda established a centralized command structure with clear lines of authority. This enabled the organization to plan and execute high-profile attacks, such as the September 11 attacks in 2001. However, the hierarchical nature of Al-Qaeda also made it susceptible to disruptions caused by the capture or killing of key leaders. Following bin Laden's death in 2011, the group's operational capacity was significantly weakened, highlighting the fragility of centralized terrorist organizations.

In contrast, networked terrorist groups operate through a decentralized web of loosely connected nodes. These nodes can include individuals, small groups, or even other organizations that share similar goals and methodologies. The networked structure allows for greater flexibility and resilience, as the loss of any single node does not necessarily compromise the entire network. This makes networked groups more difficult to dismantle compared to their hierarchical counterparts. However, coordination and communication within networked structures can be challenging, potentially leading to inconsistencies in strategy and execution.

The Islamic State (ISIS) exemplifies a networked terrorist organization. While it initially operated under a more centralized structure when it controlled large swathes of territory in Iraq and Syria, ISIS has since adapted to a more diffuse network model. This shift has enabled it to maintain a presence in various regions through affiliated groups and lone actors who carry out attacks in its name. The networked structure has allowed ISIS to continue its operations despite significant territorial losses and leadership decimation.

Cellular terrorist groups represent another organizational type, characterized by small, autonomous cells that operate independently of one another. Each cell typically consists of a handful of members who are often unaware of the identities or activities of other cells. This compartmentalization enhances operational security, as the capture or compromise of one cell does not lead to the exposure of the entire organization. Cellular structures are particularly effective for conducting covert operations and evading detection by security forces.

The Provisional Irish Republican Army (PIRA) is an example of a cellular terrorist organization. The PIRA employed a cell structure to carry out its campaign against British rule in Northern Ireland. By limiting the knowledge of its members to their specific cell, the PIRA reduced the risk of widespread infiltration and maintained operational secrecy. This approach enabled the group to sustain its activities over an extended period, despite intense counterterrorism efforts by British security forces.

Leaderless resistance is a more recent and unconventional organizational model that eschews formal hierarchies and centralized command structures. Instead, it relies on autonomous individuals or small groups who are inspired by a common ideology or cause but operate independently. These individuals or groups may be motivated by propaganda and guidance disseminated through media channels, but they plan and execute their actions without direct oversight or coordination from a central leadership. Leaderless resistance is highly resilient to traditional counterterrorism measures, as there are no leaders to target or networks to disrupt.

The concept of leaderless resistance has been advocated by various right-wing extremist movements. For instance, the "lone wolf" attacks carried out by individuals inspired by white supremacist or anti-government ideologies exemplify this model. These attackers often act without direct orders from any organization, making it difficult for authorities to anticipate or prevent their actions. The decentralized and spontaneous nature of leaderless resistance poses significant challenges for law enforcement and intelligence agencies, as traditional methods of surveillance and disruption are less effective against such diffuse threats.

Each type of terrorist organizational structure has its own strengths and weaknesses, shaped by the specific context in which the group operates. Hierarchical organizations benefit from clear leadership and coordinated planning but are vulnerable to leadership targeting. Networked groups gain resilience and adaptability but face challenges in maintaining consistent strategy and communication. Cellular structures offer operational security and stealth but can be limited in scale and scope. Leaderless resistance maximizes individual autonomy and evades traditional counterterrorism tactics but can result in unpredictable and indiscriminate violence.

Understanding the organizational structures of terrorist groups is crucial for developing effective counterterrorism strategies. By analyzing how these groups are organized, policymakers and security professionals can tailor their approaches to disrupt and dismantle terrorist networks more effectively. For instance, strategies to counter hierarchical organizations might focus on leadership targeting and intelligence gathering to disrupt command and control. Countering networked groups may require efforts to identify and map out connections between nodes and disrupt communication channels. Cellular organizations might be combated through infiltration and surveillance to uncover and neutralize individual cells. Addressing leaderless resistance may involve counter-messaging to undermine ideological motivations and community engagement to prevent radicalization. Hierarchical, networked, cellular, and leaderless resistance models each present unique operational dynamics and challenges. A nuanced understanding of these structures enables more effective counterterrorism strategies, ultimately enhancing the ability to prevent and respond to terrorist threats. As terrorist groups continue to adapt and innovate, ongoing analysis and adaptation of counterterrorism approaches remain essential to maintaining security and stability.

The hierarchy and leadership of terrorist groups

The hierarchical structure generally consists of several tiers. At the top is the senior leadership, which includes the emir or commander-in-chief and a small circle of trusted advisors or a shura council. This tier is responsible for long-term planning, high-level strategy, and maintaining the group's ideological coherence. They are also tasked with securing funding and resources, often through illicit means such as extortion, drug trafficking, or donations from sympathetic individuals and organizations. The senior leadership maintains a certain degree of separation from the operational aspects to ensure their safety and the continuity of the group's leadership.

Below the senior leadership is the mid-level command, which includes regional commanders and operational planners. These individuals are responsible for translating the strategic directives of the senior leadership into actionable plans. They oversee the execution of operations, coordinate between different cells or units, and ensure that resources are allocated efficiently. This tier is crucial for maintaining the operational tempo and adapting to changing circumstances on the ground. The mid-level command often operates in a decentralized manner, with regional commanders given significant autonomy to make tactical decisions based on their local knowledge and expertise.

The base of the hierarchy is composed of the foot soldiers or operatives who carry out the actual attacks and other activities. These individuals are often recruited based on their ideological commitment, skills, or local connections. They receive training in various aspects of terrorism, including bomb-making, weapons handling, and covert operations. The foot soldiers are the most visible and vulnerable part of the organization, as they are the ones who directly engage with the enemy and bear the brunt of counter-terrorism efforts. Their effectiveness is largely dependent on the quality of training and the level of support they receive from the higher echelons of the hierarchy.

Leadership in terrorist groups is not static; it evolves in response to internal dynamics and external pressures. The death or capture of a leader can have a significant impact on the group's operations and morale. Succession planning is therefore a critical aspect of leadership. In some cases, leadership transitions are smooth, with a clear line of succession and a well-prepared successor. In other cases, the transition can be fraught with power struggles and infighting, which can weaken the group and create opportunities for defections or splintering.

The ideological commitment of the leadership is a key factor in the cohesion and resilience of terrorist groups. Leaders often justify their actions through a radical interpretation of religious, political, or social doctrines, which serves to legitimize their violence and attract recruits. This ideological framework is disseminated through various means, including propaganda, training materials, and direct communication with recruits. The leaders' ability to articulate a compelling vision and maintain the loyalty of their followers is essential for the group's survival and operational success.

The relationship between the leadership and the rank-and-file members is also shaped by the group's operational environment. In conflicts where terrorist groups control territory, the leadership may adopt a more centralized and hierarchical structure to govern the population and manage resources. Conversely, in environments where the group is constantly on the move or under intense pressure from security forces, a more decentralized and fluid structure may be adopted to enhance operational security and resilience.

The effectiveness of leadership in terrorist groups is also influenced by external factors such as international counter-terrorism efforts, alliances with other groups, and the geopolitical context. Leaders must navigate a complex landscape of alliances and rivalries, balancing the need for external support with the imperative of maintaining operational independence. The ability to forge strategic alliances while avoiding becoming overly dependent on external patrons is a critical skill for terrorist leaders. The senior leadership provides strategic direction and ideological guidance, while the mid-level command translates these directives into actionable plans. The foot soldiers carry out the actual operations, relying on the training and support provided by the higher tiers of the hierarchy. The leadership's ideological commitment, adaptability, and ability to navigate complex external dynamics are key factors in the group's success and survival. Understanding the nuances of terrorist leadership and organizational structure is essential for developing effective counter-terrorism strategies.

The recruitment and training of terrorists

Recruitment strategies vary widely depending on the group's ideology, resources, and operational environment. Some groups, like Al-Qaeda and ISIS, have leveraged the internet and social media to cast a wide net, appealing to individuals across the globe through propaganda that romanticizes jihad and promises a sense of adventure and heroism. These online platforms serve not only as recruitment tools but also as virtual training grounds where potential recruits can access a wealth of information on bomb-making, combat tactics, and ideological justifications for violence. In contrast, more localized groups might rely on personal networks, community infiltration, and face-to-face interactions to identify and recruit members. This method allows for a more personal touch, exploiting existing social bonds and grievances to draw individuals into the group.

Once identified, potential recruits undergo a process of assessment and indoctrination. This phase is crucial as it serves to solidify the individual's commitment to the group's cause and erode any moral or ethical reservations they might have about engaging in violence. Indoctrination often involves intensive religious or ideological study, coupled with exposure to the group's propaganda and narratives that depict the enemy as inherently evil and the group's actions as necessary and justified. The process is designed to create a binary worldview where the recruit sees only two options: join the group and fight for the cause or remain passive and complicit in the perceived injustices.

Training is the next critical phase, where recruits are physically and psychologically prepared for their roles within the organization. The nature and intensity of training can vary significantly based on the group's objectives and operational needs. For instance, groups focused on insurgency or guerrilla warfare may prioritize physical conditioning, weapons handling, and combat tactics. In contrast, groups with a more clandestine or terrorist focus might emphasize skills such as bomb-making, covert communication, and surveillance evasion. Training camps, often located in remote or lawless regions, provide an environment where recruits can be isolated from external influences and subjected to rigorous physical and psychological conditioning. These camps serve not only to build technical skills but also to foster a strong sense of camaraderie and loyalty among the recruits, further binding them to the group.

Psychological manipulation plays a significant role throughout the recruitment and training process. Terrorist organizations employ various techniques to break down the individual's existing identity and rebuild it in alignment with the group's ideology. This can include the use of intense indoctrination sessions, sleep deprivation, and stress positions, all designed to weaken the recruit's resistance and make them more pliable to the group's demands. The creation of an "us versus them" mentality is also a common tactic, where recruits are made to feel part of an elite group with a special mission, set apart from the rest of society.

The role of leadership in recruitment and training cannot be overstated. Charismatic leaders often act as the glue that holds the organization together, providing a unifying vision and rallying point for recruits. These leaders are adept at exploiting psychological vulnerabilities, offering a sense of purpose and belonging that many recruits may feel is lacking in their lives. Leaders also play a crucial role in maintaining morale and cohesion within the group, particularly in the face of setbacks or external pressure. Their ability to inspire and motivate can be a decisive factor in the group's ability to sustain its operations and achieve its objectives.

The organizational structure of terrorist groups also influences recruitment and training strategies. Hierarchical groups with clear command structures may have more formalized recruitment and training programs, with specialized units responsible for identifying and indoctrinating new members. In contrast, more decentralized or networked groups might rely on a more fluid and adaptive approach, leveraging personal relationships and local networks to recruit and train members. The structure of the group can also impact its resilience and ability to withstand external pressures. Hierarchical groups may be more vulnerable to decapitation strikes that target key leaders, while decentralized groups might be more resilient but also more difficult to eradicate due to their diffuse nature.

The role of technology in recruitment and training has become increasingly significant in the modern era. The internet and social media have revolutionized the way terrorist groups operate, enabling them to reach a global audience with unprecedented ease. Online platforms serve not only as tools for propaganda and recruitment but also as virtual training grounds where recruits can access a wealth of information and connect with like-minded individuals. This digital landscape presents both opportunities and challenges for counter-terrorism efforts. While it allows for more effective monitoring and disruption of terrorist activities, it also provides terrorists with new avenues for recruitment and radicalization that are harder to detect and counter.

The impact of recruitment and training on the effectiveness and longevity of terrorist groups is profound. Effective recruitment ensures a steady supply of new members, while rigorous training equips them with the skills and mindset needed to carry out operations. However, the process is not without its challenges. Effective counter-terrorism measures can disrupt recruitment networks, target training camps, and undermine the ideological appeal of terrorist groups. Additionally, internal dynamics such as factionalism, leadership disputes, and operational setbacks can also impact the recruitment and training process, potentially weakening the group over time.

Understanding the recruitment and training processes of terrorist groups is crucial for developing effective counter-terrorism strategies. By identifying and targeting the mechanisms through which terrorist organizations attract and prepare new members, it is possible to disrupt their operations and reduce their capacity for violence. This requires a multifaceted approach that combines intelligence gathering, psychological operations, and targeted interventions aimed at disrupting the recruitment and training pipeline. It also necessitates a deep understanding of the social, psychological, and ideological factors that drive individuals to join terrorist groups, allowing for the development of more effective prevention and intervention strategies. By understanding these processes, it is possible to develop more effective counter-terrorism strategies that address the root causes of radicalization and disrupt the mechanisms through which terrorist groups sustain and expand their operations. This requires a nuanced approach that combines intelligence, psychology, and strategic intervention to undermine the appeal and operational capacity of terrorist organizations.

Chapter 4: The Tactics and Strategies of Terrorism

The different types of terrorist attacks

Bombings are one of the most common forms of terrorist attacks, characterized by their ability to cause widespread destruction and fear with a single, often highly coordinated, explosion. The choice of target, timing, and location are critical factors in maximizing the impact of a bombing. Terrorists often select densely populated areas or symbolic sites to inflict maximum casualties and garner extensive media coverage. The psychological impact of bombings is profound, as they create an atmosphere of fear and uncertainty, undermining public confidence in security measures. The materials used in bombings can range from homemade explosives to sophisticated devices, reflecting the technical capabilities and resources of the terrorist group. The strategic goal of bombings is not only to cause immediate physical damage but also to send a powerful message to both the target audience and the broader public, often with the intent of influencing political or social change.

Shootings, another prevalent form of terrorist attack, involve the use of firearms to kill or injure individuals in a targeted or indiscriminate manner. Unlike bombings, shootings often require a more direct and personal engagement from the attackers. This type of attack can be carried out by a single individual or a group, and the choice of weaponry can vary significantly, from handguns to automatic rifles. The tactical advantage of shootings lies in their potential for mobility and adaptability, allowing terrorists to change targets quickly and evade law enforcement. The psychological impact of shootings is also significant, as they can create a sense of vulnerability and helplessness among the public. The choice of location for shootings is often strategic, targeting places where people feel safe, such as schools, shopping centers, or places of worship, to amplify the shock and horror of the attack. The primary objective of shootings is usually to instill fear, disrupt normalcy, and draw attention to the terrorists' cause.

Hijackings, typically involving airplanes, ships, or other forms of transportation, are a dramatic form of terrorist attack that garners significant international attention. The strategic advantage of hijackings lies in their ability to seize control of valuable assets and hold them hostage, creating a high-stakes crisis situation. The psychological impact of hijackings is substantial, as they involve the direct threat to human lives and can lead to protracted negotiations and standoffs. The targets of hijackings are often chosen for their symbolic value or their potential to cause widespread disruption. For example, hijacking an airplane not only endangers the lives of passengers and crew but also disrupts air travel and international commerce. The goals of hijackings can vary, from making political demands to seeking ransom or publicity. The success of counterterrorism efforts in preventing hijackings depends on robust security measures, intelligence gathering, and international cooperation.

Kidnappings are a more targeted form of terrorist attack, involving the abduction of individuals to be held for ransom, used as leverage in negotiations, or as a means of drawing attention to specific demands. The victims of kidnappings can range from ordinary civilians to high-profile figures, such as politicians, journalists, or aid workers. The strategic use of kidnappings allows terrorists to exert pressure on governments, organizations, or communities to meet their demands, which can include financial payments, the release of prisoners, or changes in policy. The psychological impact of kidnappings is severe, as they create a climate of fear and anxiety, with the constant threat of violence hanging over the victims and their families. The duration of kidnappings can vary, from short-term abductions to long-term captivity, depending on the terrorists' objectives and the responses of the authorities. Effective counterterrorism strategies for addressing kidnappings involve a combination of intelligence operations, negotiation tactics, and, in some cases, military intervention.

Cyber-attacks represent a modern and increasingly prevalent form of terrorism, leveraging technology to disrupt, damage, or gain unauthorized access to computer systems and networks. The targets of cyber-attacks can include critical infrastructure, financial institutions, government agencies, and private companies. The tactics used in cyber-attacks can range from hacking and malware deployment to denial-of-service attacks and data breaches. The strategic advantage of cyber-attacks lies in their ability to cause widespread disruption and economic damage with relatively low risk to the attackers. The psychological impact of cyber-attacks is also significant, as they can erode public trust in digital security and create a sense of vulnerability in an increasingly interconnected world. The goals of cyber-attacks can vary, from financial gain and political activism to espionage and sabotage. Counterterrorism efforts in the realm of cyber-security require a multifaceted approach, including robust defensive measures, proactive threat detection, and international collaboration to address the transnational nature of cyber threats.

Biological and chemical attacks involve the use of toxic substances or pathogens to inflict harm on individuals or populations. These types of attacks are particularly dangerous due to their potential to cause mass casualties and widespread panic. The tactics used in biological and chemical attacks can include the dissemination of agents through air, water, or contaminated objects. The strategic advantage of these attacks lies in their ability to bypass traditional security measures and create a delayed but devastating impact. The psychological impact of biological and chemical attacks is profound, as they evoke fear of invisible threats and undermine public confidence in safety and health systems. The targets of these attacks can be diverse, ranging from crowded public spaces to military installations or critical infrastructure. The goals of biological and chemical attacks are often to cause mass disruption, instill fear, and potentially influence political or social outcomes. Counterterrorism strategies for these types of attacks require specialized knowledge and capabilities, including threat detection, decontamination procedures, and medical response plans to mitigate the effects of exposure.

In addition to these primary categories, terrorist attacks can also take the form of arson, vehicular attacks, and improvised explosive device (IED) attacks. Arson involves the deliberate setting of fires to cause destruction and fear, often targeting symbolic buildings or areas with high foot traffic. Vehicular attacks, where terrorists use vehicles as weapons to ram into crowds, have become more common in recent years due to their relative ease of execution and potential for high casualties. IED attacks, which involve the use of homemade bombs or explosive devices, can be deployed in various settings, from urban environments to conflict zones. The strategic use of these tactics reflects the adaptability and resourcefulness of terrorist groups in exploiting vulnerabilities and maximizing impact. The psychological effects of these attacks are significant, as they create an environment of unpredictability and fear. Counterterrorism efforts must continually evolve to address these emerging tactics and enhance preventive measures.

The diversity of terrorist attack tactics underscores the complexity of counterterrorism efforts. Each type of attack requires a tailored response, taking into account the specific characteristics and objectives of the terrorists involved. Effective counterterrorism strategies must integrate intelligence gathering, proactive security measures, public awareness campaigns, and international cooperation to address the multifaceted nature of the threat. Additionally, understanding the psychological dimensions of terrorism is crucial in developing strategies that not only prevent attacks but also mitigate their impact on society. By comprehensively analyzing the tactics and strategies of terrorism, it is possible to develop more resilient and adaptive approaches to safeguarding public safety and security.

The ever-evolving landscape of terrorism necessitates ongoing research and analysis to stay ahead of emerging threats. Terrorist groups continually adapt their tactics to exploit new technologies, vulnerabilities, and societal changes. For example, the rise of social media has provided terrorists with new platforms for recruitment, propaganda, and coordination. The use of encrypted communication channels and the dark web has also enabled terrorists to operate with greater anonymity and security. As such, counterterrorism efforts must incorporate advanced technological tools and innovative approaches to monitor, analyze, and disrupt terrorist activities. Collaboration between governments, private sector entities, and international organizations is essential in creating a unified and effective response to the global threat of terrorism. Understanding the tactical and psychological dimensions of bombings, shootings, hijackings, kidnappings, cyber-attacks, and biological or chemical attacks is essential for developing comprehensive and effective responses. By staying informed about the evolving tactics of terrorism and enhancing collaborative efforts, it is possible to mitigate the threats posed by terrorist groups and protect the safety and security of societies worldwide.

The targets of terrorist attacks

In addition to political targets, terrorists frequently target civilian populations, particularly in crowded places such as markets, transportation hubs, and public events. The primary objective here is to cause widespread fear and panic, disrupt daily life, and erode the sense of security among the general public. These attacks are designed to be indiscriminate, affecting a broad cross-section of society, which serves to amplify the psychological impact. The randomness and unpredictability of these attacks heighten the sense of vulnerability and helplessness among the population, which can lead to significant social and economic repercussions. The media coverage that ensues from such attacks further propagates the terrorists' agenda, spreading fear and anxiety far beyond the immediate vicinity of the incident.

Religious sites and gatherings are also common targets for terrorist attacks. These locations are chosen not only for their symbolic significance but also for the potential to incite sectarian violence and deepen religious divides. Attacks on places of worship or religious events can provoke retaliatory violence, leading to a cycle of reprisals and counter-reprisals that exacerbate communal tensions. This strategy is particularly effective in regions with existing religious or sectarian conflicts, where such attacks can inflame passions and escalate violence. The intent behind targeting religious sites is often to exploit and deepen existing divides, thereby destabilizing society and undermining social cohesion.

Economic targets, such as financial institutions, industrial complexes, and critical infrastructure, are also prime targets for terrorist attacks. The aim here is to inflict economic damage, disrupt essential services, and undermine economic stability. By targeting key economic assets, terrorists seek to weaken the financial foundations of a state, create economic uncertainty, and potentially influence government policies or actions. These attacks can have far-reaching consequences, affecting not only the immediate vicinity but also broader economic systems and international markets. The disruption of critical infrastructure, such as power grids or transportation networks, can have cascading effects, impacting various sectors and exacerbating the overall impact of the attack.

Cultural and heritage sites are another category of targets that terrorists frequently focus on. These sites hold significant historical, cultural, and emotional value for communities and nations. By destroying or damaging these sites, terrorists aim to erase cultural identity, undermine historical continuity, and provoke outrage both domestically and internationally. Such attacks are often intended to send a powerful message about the terrorists' disdain for the targeted culture or civilization and their willingness to destroy irreplaceable symbols of heritage. The global outcry and media attention generated by such acts of destruction further serve to amplify the terrorists' message and highlight their capability to strike at the heart of cultural identity.

Terrorists also increasingly target symbols of Western influence and modernity, such as hotels, shopping malls, and entertainment venues. These targets are chosen for their representation of globalization, capitalism, and Western cultural influence. Attacks on these sites are intended to challenge the spread of Western values and lifestyles, provoke a reaction against Western presence and influence, and rally support from those who oppose Westernization. The choice of these targets reflects a broader ideological struggle, where terrorists seek to resist and undermine the pervasive influence of Western culture and ideas. The impact of these attacks is often magnified by the international nature of the targets, affecting not only local populations but also international visitors and stakeholders.

In recent years, terrorists have also shown a growing interest in targeting soft targets, which are characterized by their lack of security and ease of access. These can include public spaces, educational institutions, and healthcare facilities. The rationale behind targeting such locations is the ease of carrying out an attack with minimal risk of interception or prevention. Soft targets are chosen to exploit vulnerabilities and maximize casualties, thereby creating a heightened sense of fear and insecurity. The indiscriminate nature of these attacks, coupled with the difficulty of protecting such locations comprehensively, makes them particularly appealing to terrorists seeking to demonstrate their reach and capability.

The strategic selection of targets is also influenced by the desire to achieve specific political or ideological goals. For instance, terrorists may target international organizations, diplomatic missions, or foreign businesses to express opposition to foreign policies, interventions, or economic interests. These attacks are intended to convey a message of defiance and resistance, often aimed at influencing international perceptions and actions. By attacking entities associated with foreign powers, terrorists seek to draw international attention to their cause, garner support from sympathetic groups, and potentially influence the policies or actions of the targeted foreign entities.

Furthermore, terrorists often select targets based on the potential for high-profile media coverage. The media plays a crucial role in amplifying the impact of terrorist attacks, spreading fear and anxiety, and shaping public perception. Terrorists are acutely aware of the power of media coverage and often plan their attacks to maximize exposure and sensationalism. The choice of targets that guarantee extensive media coverage ensures that the terrorists' message reaches a wide audience, thereby enhancing the psychological impact and propagating fear beyond the immediate victims. This symbiotic relationship between terrorism and media underscores the importance of responsible reporting and the need to balance the public's right to know with the potential for amplifying terrorist propaganda.

The selection of targets is also influenced by the terrorists' operational capabilities and resources. While some groups may possess the means to carry out complex, large-scale attacks, others may focus on smaller, more manageable targets that still achieve significant impact. The choice of targets is thus a reflection of the terrorists' strategic goals, operational constraints, and the resources at their disposal. Understanding the interplay between these factors is essential for developing effective counter-terrorism strategies that address the root causes of terrorism, disrupt terrorist networks, and mitigate the threat posed by these groups. By understanding the rationale behind the selection of these targets, we can gain deeper insights into the tactics and strategies of terrorist organizations. This knowledge is crucial for developing comprehensive counter-terrorism measures that address the multifaceted nature of the terrorist threat. Effective counter-terrorism efforts must consider the diverse range of targets, the underlying motivations for their selection, and the broader implications of these attacks on society and international relations. Through a nuanced understanding of terrorist targets and the strategies behind their selection, we can better equip ourselves to prevent and respond to terrorist threats, safeguarding the security and well-being of communities worldwide.

The impact of terrorist attacks

The economic consequences of terrorist attacks are equally significant, often leading to substantial financial losses for individuals, businesses, and governments. The immediate costs include damage to infrastructure, property, and the loss of human lives, which can strain local and national economies. In the longer term, the economic impact extends to reduced tourism, decreased foreign investment, and increased security expenditures. Tourism, a vital sector for many economies, often suffers greatly following terrorist attacks due to safety concerns. Investors may also become wary of committing capital to regions perceived as high-risk, further stifling economic growth. Additionally, governments are compelled to allocate substantial resources to enhance security measures, diverting funds from other critical areas such as education, healthcare, and social services. These economic strains can exacerbate existing social inequalities and contribute to a cycle of poverty and marginalization, particularly in regions already struggling with economic challenges.

Politically, terrorist attacks can provoke significant shifts in policy and governance. Governments often respond to terrorism by implementing stricter security measures, which can include increased surveillance, enhanced border controls, and the expansion of law enforcement powers. While these measures aim to protect citizens and prevent future attacks, they can also lead to a curtailment of civil liberties and human rights. The balance between security and freedom is delicate, and the imposition of stringent security protocols can foster a climate of suspicion and fear. the political discourse surrounding terrorism often becomes highly polarized, with debates over the appropriate response to terrorism reflecting broader ideological divides. This polarization can undermine democratic processes and erode public trust in institutions.

The media plays a crucial role in shaping public perception of terrorist attacks. Extensive media coverage can amplify the psychological impact of terrorism, spreading fear and anxiety far beyond the immediate vicinity of the attack. The way terrorist acts are reported can influence public opinion and policy responses, sometimes leading to an overestimation of the threat and a disproportionate focus on security measures. Sensationalist media coverage can also contribute to the spread of misinformation and stereotypes, particularly against specific ethnic or religious groups. This can fuel prejudice and discrimination, further dividing communities and complicating efforts to address the root causes of terrorism.

In terms of social dynamics, terrorist attacks can reinforce existing social divisions and create new ones. Acts of terrorism often target symbols of power and normalcy, such as government buildings, transportation hubs, and public spaces. By striking at these symbols, terrorists aim to disrupt societal order and provoke a reaction. The ensuing response, whether it involves military

41

action, policy changes, or community vigilance, can alter social interactions and community cohesion. In some cases, the fear of terrorism can lead to the stigmatization and marginalization of certain groups, particularly those perceived to share characteristics with the perpetrators. This marginalization can exacerbate social tensions and contribute to cycles of violence and retribution.

The impact of terrorist attacks on international relations is also significant. Acts of terrorism can strain diplomatic relations, particularly when attacks are attributed to groups based in other countries. Governments may respond with sanctions, military interventions, or increased diplomatic pressure on countries perceived to harbor terrorists. These actions can escalate tensions and contribute to international conflicts. Additionally, international cooperation in combating terrorism often involves complex negotiations and compromises, as countries seek to balance their national security interests with broader geopolitical considerations. The global nature of terrorism necessitates collaboration across borders, yet differing national priorities and approaches can complicate these efforts.

The psychological impact of terrorism extends beyond the immediate victims to encompass broader societal changes. The constant threat of terrorism can lead to a pervasive sense of insecurity, influencing how individuals perceive risk and make decisions. This heightened sense of vulnerability can affect various aspects of life, from personal choices regarding travel and public gatherings to broader societal attitudes towards privacy and security. The normalization of heightened security measures can lead to a gradual acceptance of surveillance and restrictions on personal freedoms as necessary evils. This shift in societal norms can have long-term implications for democratic values and individual rights.

The economic ramifications of terrorism are not evenly distributed, often disproportionately affecting certain sectors and populations. Small businesses, which may lack the resources to invest in enhanced security measures, can be particularly vulnerable to the economic fallout of terrorist attacks. Similarly, workers in the tourism and hospitality industries may face job losses and reduced income due to declining demand. The economic disparities exacerbated by terrorism can lead to increased social unrest and a sense of injustice, further complicating efforts to foster social cohesion and stability. Governments and international organizations must therefore adopt comprehensive approaches that address both the immediate and long-term economic impacts of terrorism, ensuring that support is provided to those most affected.

The political landscape is also reshaped by the threat of terrorism, with governments often adopting more authoritarian measures in the name of security. The balance between protecting citizens and preserving civil liberties is a central challenge in the fight against terrorism. Policies that expand surveillance and restrict freedoms can lead to a climate of fear and suspicion, undermining democratic principles. The erosion of civil liberties can have a chilling effect on political dissent and activism, as individuals and groups become wary of attracting scrutiny from security agencies. This dynamic can stifle innovation and limit the robust exchange of ideas necessary for a healthy democracy.

The role of media in the context of terrorism is a double-edged sword. While responsible journalism can inform and educate the public, sensationalist coverage can exacerbate fear and misunderstanding. The media's portrayal of terrorist attacks can influence public perception and policy responses, highlighting the need for accurate and nuanced reporting. Ethical considerations in media coverage include the need to avoid glorifying terrorists or their actions, which can inadvertently serve as a form of propaganda. Media organizations have a responsibility to provide context and analysis, helping the public understand the complex factors underlying terrorism without contributing to hysteria or prejudice.

Socially, the aftermath of terrorist attacks can lead to increased solidarity and community resilience, but it can also deepen existing divides. Acts of terrorism often prompt an outpouring of support and unity among affected communities, as individuals come together to support victims and reaffirm shared values. However, the fear and uncertainty generated by terrorism can also lead to scapegoating and the targeting of minority groups. Efforts to build resilient communities must therefore focus on fostering inclusivity and addressing the underlying social and economic factors that contribute to vulnerability and marginalization. Community-based initiatives, such as interfaith dialogues and cultural exchange programs, can play a crucial role in bridging divides and promoting mutual understanding.

In the international arena, the fight against terrorism necessitates robust cooperation and coordination among countries. Terrorism is a transnational threat that requires collective action to address effectively. International agreements and organizations, such as the United Nations, play a vital role in facilitating cooperation on counterterrorism efforts. However, differing national priorities and approaches can pose challenges to effective collaboration. Balancing national security interests with respect for international law and human rights is a complex task. Effective international cooperation requires dialogue, trust-building, and a commitment to shared goals, recognizing that terrorism is a common enemy that transcends national borders.

The psychological toll of terrorism on individuals and communities underscores the need for comprehensive mental health support and resilience-building initiatives. Addressing the psychological impact of terrorism involves not only immediate crisis intervention but also long-term support for those affected. Mental health services must be accessible and culturally sensitive, recognizing the diverse needs of different populations. Community-based approaches that involve local leaders and organizations can enhance the effectiveness of mental health interventions, fostering a sense of ownership and trust. Resilience-building efforts should also focus on strengthening social networks and support systems, helping communities to recover and adapt in the face of adversity.

The economic strategies for mitigating the impact of terrorism involve a combination of immediate relief and long-term investment. Governments and international organizations must provide financial support to affected individuals and businesses, helping them to recover and rebuild. Long-term economic strategies should focus on enhancing resilience through diversification and innovation. Investing in infrastructure, education, and technology can create new opportunities and reduce dependency on vulnerable sectors. Policies that promote social and economic inclusion are also essential, ensuring that the benefits of growth are widely shared and that vulnerable populations are not left behind.

The political response to terrorism must balance security with the protection of democratic values. While it is imperative to prevent future attacks, measures that erode civil liberties can ultimately undermine the fabric of society. Effective counterterrorism policies should be based on evidence and respect for human rights, ensuring that security measures are proportionate and targeted. Public engagement and transparency in the development of counterterrorism strategies are crucial, fostering trust and cooperation between governments and citizens. Democratic institutions must be safeguarded, ensuring that the fight against terrorism does not come at the expense of fundamental freedoms and rights. The psychological, economic, political, and social consequences of terrorism are interrelated and complex, requiring comprehensive and coordinated responses. Addressing the root causes of terrorism, fostering resilience, and promoting social cohesion are essential components of an effective counterterrorism strategy. By understanding the multifaceted nature of terrorism and its far-reaching impacts, societies can develop more nuanced and effective approaches to preventing and responding to this persistent threat.

Chapter 5: The Counterterrorism Response

The different types of counterterrorism measures

In addition to physical security measures, counterterrorism efforts heavily rely on intelligence gathering and analysis. Intelligence agencies play a crucial role in identifying and tracking terrorist networks, uncovering their plans, and disrupting their operations before they can execute attacks. This involves extensive surveillance, the use of informants, and the analysis of communications and financial transactions. The integration of advanced technologies, such as data mining and artificial intelligence, has significantly enhanced the capabilities of intelligence agencies to detect patterns and predict potential threats. Effective intelligence sharing between national and international agencies is also paramount, as terrorism is often a transnational phenomenon requiring coordinated efforts across borders.

Legislative measures form another critical component of counterterrorism strategies. Governments enact laws and regulations that provide the legal framework for counterterrorism operations, including the authorization of surveillance, the detention of suspects, and the prosecution of individuals involved in terrorist activities. These laws often balance the need for security with the protection of civil liberties, a delicate equilibrium that reflects the values of democratic societies. Specialized courts and legal procedures may be established to handle terrorism-related cases, ensuring that they are dealt with swiftly and effectively while upholding the principles of justice.

Military intervention represents a more overt and direct approach to counterterrorism, particularly when terrorist groups control territory or pose a significant threat to national or international security. Military operations can range from targeted airstrikes and Special Forces missions to broader campaigns aimed at dismantling terrorist infrastructures and support networks. These operations are often conducted in collaboration with international coalitions, reflecting the global nature of the terrorist threat. The use of military force must be carefully calibrated to avoid civilian casualties and collateral damage, which can undermine legitimacy and fuel further radicalization.

Counterterrorism also extends to the financial realm, where measures are implemented to disrupt the funding of terrorist activities. Financial intelligence units monitor and investigate suspicious transactions, while international cooperation ensures the enforcement of sanctions against individuals and organizations linked to terrorism. By cutting off the financial lifelines of terrorist groups, authorities aim to cripple their operational capabilities and reduce their capacity to carry out attacks. This aspect of counterterrorism underscores the importance of a holistic approach that addresses not only the immediate threats but also the underlying support systems that sustain terrorist activities.

Psychological and ideological countermeasures are equally important in the fight against terrorism. Efforts to counter radicalization and extremist ideologies involve community engagement, education, and the promotion of alternative narratives that challenge the appeal of terrorism. Governments and non-governmental organizations work to build resilience within communities, empowering individuals to resist radicalization and fostering a sense of belonging and purpose that can mitigate the vulnerabilities exploited by terrorist recruiters. These initiatives highlight the importance of addressing the root causes of terrorism, such as social alienation, economic deprivation, and political grievances.

Technological advancements have also introduced new tools and methods for counterterrorism. The use of biometrics, facial recognition, and drone technology has enhanced the ability to monitor and respond to threats in real-time. Social media platforms are increasingly monitored to identify and counter online radicalization efforts, while encryption and cybersecurity measures protect critical infrastructure and sensitive information from cyber-attacks. The integration of technology in counterterrorism efforts reflects the evolving nature of the threat and the need for innovative solutions to stay ahead of adversaries.

International cooperation is a cornerstone of effective counterterrorism. Multilateral agreements and organizations, such as the United Nations and INTERPOL, facilitate the sharing of intelligence, best practices, and resources among nations. Joint training exercises and collaborative operations enhance the capabilities of national security forces, while diplomatic efforts work to address the root causes of terrorism and promote stability in regions prone to conflict and extremism. The global nature of terrorism necessitates a unified and coordinated response, transcending national boundaries and leveraging the collective strength of the international community.

Preventive measures focus on addressing the conditions conducive to terrorism, such as poverty, lack of education, and political instability. Development programs aimed at improving socio-economic conditions can reduce the appeal of extremist ideologies and create opportunities for individuals to pursue productive and fulfilling lives. Political reforms that promote inclusivity, justice, and good governance can mitigate the grievances that fuel radicalization. By addressing these underlying issues, preventive measures seek to create an environment in which terrorism is less likely to take root and flourish.

Crisis management and response strategies are essential components of counterterrorism efforts. In the event of a terrorist attack, a well-coordinated response can minimize casualties, manage public panic, and restore order. This involves the rapid deployment of emergency services, the establishment of secure perimeters, and effective communication with the public and media. Post-incident investigations and debriefings help to identify lessons learned and improve future response capabilities. Effective crisis management not only mitigates the immediate impact of an attack but also reinforces public confidence in the ability of authorities to protect and respond to threats.

Rehabilitation and reintegration programs are critical for addressing the aftermath of terrorism, particularly for individuals who have been involved in or affected by extremist activities. These programs aim to reintegrate former extremists into society, providing them with education, vocational training, and psychological support to facilitate their transition. Community-based approaches that involve family members, religious leaders, and local organizations can enhance the effectiveness of these programs by fostering a supportive environment for reintegration. The success of rehabilitation efforts is crucial for breaking the cycle of radicalization and reducing the long-term threat of terrorism.

The role of media and public communication in counterterrorism cannot be overstated. Responsible reporting and public awareness campaigns can help to counter extremist narratives, reduce fear and panic, and promote a balanced understanding of the threat. Governments and media organizations must work together to ensure that information is disseminated accurately and responsibly, avoiding sensationalism and misinformation that can exacerbate the situation. Public communication strategies must be carefully crafted to inform and reassure the public while maintaining transparency and accountability.

In short, the ethical dimensions of counterterrorism measures must be carefully considered. The balance between security and civil liberties is a persistent challenge, requiring ongoing scrutiny and debate. Counterterrorism efforts must be conducted within the framework of human rights and the rule of law, ensuring that measures taken do not infringe upon the fundamental freedoms and rights of individuals. Ethical considerations also extend to the treatment of detainees, the use of force, and the transparency of operations. By adhering to ethical principles, counterterrorism efforts can maintain legitimacy and public support, which are essential for their long-term success. From physical security protocols and intelligence gathering to legislative frameworks and international cooperation, these measures are designed to prevent, deter, and respond to terrorism in all its forms. The integration of advanced technologies, community engagement, and preventive strategies underscores the holistic approach required to address both the immediate and underlying causes of terrorism. Ethical considerations and the protection of civil liberties remain central to ensuring that counterterrorism efforts are effective, legitimate, and sustainable. Through a coordinated and multifaceted approach, societies can enhance their resilience and reduce the threat posed by terrorism, safeguarding the security and well-being of their citizens.

The effectiveness of counterterrorism measures

One of the primary counterterrorism measures discussed is intelligence gathering and analysis. The authors emphasize the critical role of intelligence in preempting terrorist activities. Effective intelligence operations involve a combination of human intelligence (HUMINT), signals intelligence (SIGINT), and open-source intelligence (OSINT). The integration of these various intelligence streams allows for a more comprehensive understanding of terrorist networks, their intentions, and their capabilities. The one underscores the importance of international cooperation in intelligence sharing, noting that terrorism is a transnational threat that requires a coordinated global response. The establishment of joint intelligence centers and international databases has facilitated the exchange of information, enabling countries to better anticipate and counter terrorist threats.

Another significant aspect of counterterrorism discussed in the one is the use of military force. The authors examine the role of military interventions in counterterrorism, highlighting both their potential benefits and drawbacks. On one hand, targeted military operations can disrupt terrorist activities, eliminate key leaders, and degrade the operational capacity of terrorist organizations. The use of drone strikes, special operations, and conventional military campaigns are cited as examples of how military force has been employed to combat terrorism. However, the one also acknowledges the limitations and potential negative consequences of military interventions. These include civilian casualties, collateral damage, and the potential for exacerbating anti-Western sentiments, which can fuel further radicalization and recruitment for terrorist groups. The authors argue that while military force can be an effective tool in certain contexts, it must be used judiciously and in conjunction with other non-military measures to avoid unintended consequences.

The one also explores the role of law enforcement and judicial measures in counterterrorism. Law enforcement agencies play a crucial role in investigating terrorist activities, apprehending suspects, and bringing them to justice. The authors highlight the importance of robust legal frameworks that provide law enforcement agencies with the necessary tools to combat terrorism while safeguarding civil liberties. This includes laws that criminalize terrorist activities, enable the freezing of assets, and facilitate international cooperation in extradition and mutual legal assistance. The one provides examples of successful law enforcement operations that have dismantled terrorist cells and prevented attacks. However, it also notes the challenges faced by law enforcement agencies, such as the need to balance security concerns with respect for human rights and the rule of law.

In addition to intelligence, military, and law enforcement measures, the one discusses the importance of counter-radicalization and counter-extremism strategies. These strategies focus on addressing the root causes of terrorism by countering the ideology that fuels it and preventing the radicalization of individuals. The authors outline various approaches to counter-radicalization, including community engagement, education, and counter-messaging campaigns. Community engagement involves working with local communities to build resilience against extremist ideologies and to identify individuals who may be at risk of radicalization. Education initiatives aim to promote critical thinking and tolerance, while counter-messaging campaigns seek to challenge and discredit extremist narratives. The effectiveness of these strategies is contingent on a deep understanding of the social, economic, and psychological factors that contribute to radicalization.

The one also addresses the role of technology in counterterrorism. Technological advancements have provided both opportunities and challenges in the fight against terrorism. On one hand, technologies such as biometrics, data mining, and artificial intelligence can enhance the ability of security agencies to identify and track terrorists. The use of advanced surveillance systems and predictive analytics can help preempt attacks by identifying patterns and anomalies in data. However, the one also highlights the ethical and privacy concerns associated with the use of such technologies. The balance between security and privacy is a contentious issue, with debates surrounding the extent to which governments should be allowed to monitor communications and collect data on individuals. The authors advocate for a careful and transparent approach to the use of technology in counterterrorism, one that ensures effectiveness while upholding democratic values and human rights.

Economic measures are another tool discussed in the one. The authors examine how economic sanctions, financial regulations, and efforts to disrupt terrorist financing can weaken terrorist organizations. By targeting the financial infrastructure that supports terrorism, governments can limit the resources available to terrorist groups, hindering their ability to plan and execute attacks. The one provides examples of international efforts to combat terrorist financing, such as the work of the Financial Action Task Force (FATF) and the implementation of United Nations Security Council resolutions. However, it also notes the challenges in effectively cutting off terrorist financing, given the adaptability of terrorist organizations and their ability to exploit informal financial networks.

The one further explores the impact of international cooperation and diplomacy in counterterrorism. The authors argue that terrorism is a global issue that requires a unified international response. Diplomatic efforts, such as the establishment of international conventions and protocols, play a crucial role in fostering cooperation among nations. The one highlights the importance of multilateral institutions, such as the United Nations, in coordinating global counterterrorism efforts and promoting dialogue among countries. Additionally, bilateral and regional cooperation agreements can enhance the capacity of countries to address shared terrorist threats. The authors emphasize that while international cooperation is essential, it must be underpinned by mutual trust and respect for sovereignty.

The effectiveness of counterterrorism measures is also influenced by the role of civil society and public awareness. The one discusses how civil society organizations can contribute to counterterrorism efforts by promoting social cohesion, advocating for human rights, and providing support to victims of terrorism. Public awareness campaigns can help educate the public about the nature of the terrorist threat and the importance of vigilance. The authors argue that a well-informed and engaged public can be a valuable asset in counterterrorism efforts, helping to create a resilient society that is less susceptible to extremist ideologies. It highlights the importance of a multifaceted approach that combines intelligence gathering, military force, law enforcement, counter-radicalization, technology, economic measures, international cooperation, and civil society engagement. The authors argue that while no single measure can be entirely effective on its own, a coordinated and integrated approach can significantly enhance the ability of governments and international bodies to combat terrorism. The one underscores the need for continuous adaptation and innovation in counterterrorism strategies, given the evolving nature of the terrorist threat. Ultimately, the effectiveness of counterterrorism measures depends on a balanced and nuanced approach that addresses both the immediate security concerns and the underlying factors that contribute to terrorism.

The challenges of counterterrorism

The psychological aspect of counterterrorism is equally critical and challenging. Understanding the motivations and mindset of terrorists is essential for developing effective counterterrorism strategies. However, the diversity of terrorist motivations, ranging from political grievances to religious extremism, complicates this task. Counterterrorism efforts must account for the ideological underpinnings that drive terrorist activities, as these beliefs often fuel the commitment and resilience of terrorist operatives. Addressing these motivations requires not only military and intelligence operations but also efforts to counter extremist ideologies and prevent radicalization. This necessitates a comprehensive approach that involves collaboration between governments, civil society, and international organizations to promote tolerance, inclusivity, and respect for human rights.

Another significant challenge in counterterrorism is the balance between security and civil liberties. Counterterrorism measures, such as surveillance, detention, and interrogation, often raise concerns about the infringement of individual rights and freedoms. Striking an appropriate balance between ensuring national security and upholding civil liberties is a delicate and contentious issue. Overemphasis on security can lead to authoritarian practices, erosion of democratic values, and alienation of certain communities, which may inadvertently fuel support for terrorism. Conversely, prioritizing civil liberties without adequate security measures can leave societies vulnerable to terrorist attacks. Achieving this balance requires transparent and accountable governance, robust legal frameworks, and continuous oversight to ensure that counterterrorism measures are both effective and respectful of human rights.

The global nature of terrorism adds another layer of complexity to counterterrorism efforts. Terrorist networks often operate across national borders, exploiting weak governance, porous borders, and ungoverned spaces to establish safe havens and launch attacks. This transnational dimension requires international cooperation and coordination among countries to effectively combat terrorism. However, differences in national interests, legal systems, and levels of commitment can hinder effective collaboration. The lack of a unified global strategy and the absence of universally accepted definitions of terrorism further complicate international counterterrorism efforts. Addressing these challenges necessitates the development of international norms, agreements, and frameworks that facilitate cooperation and information sharing among countries while respecting national sovereignty and legal systems.

The role of intelligence in counterterrorism cannot be overstated. Effective intelligence gathering and analysis are crucial for identifying and disrupting terrorist plots before they materialize. However, intelligence operations face numerous challenges, including the difficulty of penetrating tightly knit terrorist cells, the vast amount of data to be analyzed, and the need for timely and accurate information. The integration of advanced technologies, such as artificial intelligence and big data analytics, holds promise for enhancing intelligence capabilities. Nonetheless, these technologies also raise ethical and privacy concerns that must be carefully managed. Ensuring the effectiveness of intelligence operations while safeguarding civil liberties requires a careful balancing act and the establishment of robust oversight mechanisms.

The psychological impact of terrorism on societies is another critical challenge in counterterrorism. Terrorist attacks are designed not only to cause physical harm but also to instill fear, disrupt social cohesion, and undermine public confidence in government institutions. The psychological trauma inflicted by terrorism can have long-lasting effects on individuals and communities, leading to increased anxiety, mistrust, and social fragmentation. Counterterrorism efforts must therefore include measures to address the psychological impact of terrorism, such as providing support services for victims, promoting community resilience, and fostering social cohesion. Building resilient societies that can withstand and recover from terrorist attacks is essential for mitigating the long-term effects of terrorism.

The financial aspect of counterterrorism presents another significant challenge. Terrorist organizations require funding to sustain their operations, recruit members, and acquire resources. Disrupting the financial networks that support terrorism is crucial for weakening terrorist groups and preventing attacks. However, identifying and interdicting terrorist financing is a complex task, as terrorist organizations often use sophisticated methods to conceal their financial activities. These methods include money laundering, exploitation of informal financial systems, and the use of front companies and charities. Effective counterterrorism financing measures require international cooperation, robust regulatory frameworks, and the ability to trace and disrupt financial flows. Additionally, addressing the root causes of terrorism, such as poverty, unemployment, and lack of education, is essential for reducing the appeal of terrorist organizations and undermining their financial base.

The challenge of countering terrorist propaganda and recruitment efforts is also significant. Terrorist groups often use sophisticated propaganda to attract recruits, spread their ideology, and justify their actions. The internet and social media platforms have become powerful tools for terrorist propaganda, allowing terrorist groups to reach a global audience and recruit individuals from diverse backgrounds. Countering terrorist propaganda requires a comprehensive approach that includes not only law enforcement and intelligence efforts but also public diplomacy, strategic communications, and community engagement. Developing effective counter-narratives that challenge terrorist ideologies, promote alternative viewpoints, and highlight the destructive consequences of terrorism is essential for preventing radicalization and recruitment.

The operational challenges of counterterrorism are also considerable. Conducting counterterrorism operations, whether through military intervention, law enforcement actions, or covert operations, involves significant risks and complexities. These operations often take place in hostile environments, require precise intelligence, and involve coordination among multiple agencies and units. The potential for collateral damage, civilian casualties, and unintended consequences adds to the complexity of counterterrorism operations. Ensuring that counterterrorism operations are conducted in a manner that minimizes harm to civilians and adheres to international humanitarian law is crucial for maintaining legitimacy and public support. the success of counterterrorism operations depends on the ability to adapt to evolving threats, develop innovative tactics, and maintain the operational readiness of security forces.

The challenge of deradicalization and rehabilitation of former terrorists is an important aspect of counterterrorism efforts. Deradicalization programs aim to address the ideological motivations of terrorists and facilitate their reintegration into society. However, these programs face numerous challenges, including the difficulty of changing deeply held beliefs, the risk of recidivism, and the need for comprehensive support services. Effective deradicalization programs require a multidisciplinary approach that involves psychological counseling, education, vocational training, and community support. Ensuring the success of deradicalization efforts requires sustained investment, continuous evaluation, and adaptation to the specific needs and circumstances of individuals undergoing rehabilitation.

The role of community engagement in counterterrorism is crucial. Communities play a vital role in preventing radicalization, identifying potential threats, and supporting counterterrorism efforts. Building trust and cooperation between security forces and communities is essential for effective counterterrorism. However, mistrust, discrimination, and marginalization can undermine community engagement and hinder counterterrorism efforts. Addressing these challenges requires efforts to promote inclusivity, respect for diversity, and equal opportunities for all members of society. Empowering communities to participate in counterterrorism efforts and providing them with the resources and support needed to address local grievances and vulnerabilities is essential for building resilient societies that can effectively resist and respond to terrorism.

The ethical dimension of counterterrorism is another significant challenge. Counterterrorism measures must be conducted in a manner that upholds ethical principles and respects human rights. The use of torture, extrajudicial killings, and indiscriminate violence not only violates international law but also undermines the moral authority of counterterrorism efforts and can fuel resentment and support for terrorism. Ensuring that counterterrorism measures are conducted ethically requires the establishment of clear legal frameworks, robust oversight mechanisms, and a commitment to upholding human rights. Additionally, promoting transparency, accountability, and public discourse on counterterrorism policies is essential for maintaining public trust and legitimacy.

The technological dimension of counterterrorism presents both opportunities and challenges. Technological advancements have the potential to enhance counterterrorism capabilities, such as surveillance, intelligence gathering, and operational planning. However, terrorists also exploit technology to further their objectives, posing new challenges for counterterrorism efforts. The rapid pace of technological change requires continuous adaptation and innovation in counterterrorism strategies. Ensuring that counterterrorism efforts keep pace with technological developments while addressing the associated risks and ethical concerns is essential for maintaining effective and responsible counterterrorism practices. Addressing these challenges requires a comprehensive and dynamic approach that integrates military, intelligence, law enforcement, and community-based efforts. Developing effective counterterrorism strategies necessitates a deep understanding of the motivations and tactics of terrorist groups, the ability to adapt to evolving threats, and a commitment to upholding human rights and ethical principles. By addressing the multifaceted nature of terrorism and building resilient societies, counterterrorism efforts can effectively mitigate the threat of terrorism and promote global security and stability.

Chapter 6: The Psychology of Terrorism Victims

The trauma of terrorism

Terrorism-induced trauma often begins with an acute stress reaction, characterized by symptoms such as confusion, disorientation, and intense fear. These reactions are normal responses to an abnormal event and typically subside within a few days or weeks. However, for some individuals, these symptoms persist and develop into more severe conditions. PTSD, one of the most common outcomes of terrorist attacks, involves a prolonged period of psychological distress characterized by re-experiencing the traumatic event through flashbacks, nightmares, and intrusive thoughts. Individuals with PTSD may also exhibit avoidance behaviors, emotional numbness, and hyperarousal, significantly impacting their daily functioning and quality of life.

The psychological trauma of terrorism is not uniform across all individuals; it varies based on several factors. Proximity to the event plays a critical role; those directly affected, such as survivors and the families of victims, are at a higher risk of developing severe psychological disorders. First responders and emergency personnel, despite their training, are also highly susceptible to trauma due to their exposure to the immediate aftermath of attacks. The level of exposure, including the duration and intensity of the traumatic experience, further determines the extent of psychological impact. For instance, individuals who witnessed the event but were not physically harmed may still experience significant psychological distress due to the graphic and violent nature of terrorist acts.

Individual resilience and pre-existing mental health conditions also influence the psychological response to terrorism. Resilience, which encompasses an individual's ability to adapt and recover from adverse experiences, varies widely among people. Factors contributing to resilience include strong social support networks, effective coping strategies, and positive personality traits such as optimism and self-efficacy. Conversely, individuals with pre-existing mental health issues, such as anxiety or depression, may find their symptoms exacerbated by the trauma of terrorism. The interplay between resilience and vulnerability underscores the complex nature of trauma and highlights the need for tailored psychological interventions.

The social and cultural context in which terrorism occurs also shapes the psychological impact on victims. Societal reactions to terrorism, including media coverage and public discourse, can either mitigate or exacerbate the trauma experienced by individuals. Media sensationalism and the constant replaying of graphic images can retraumatize victims and heighten public anxiety. On the other hand, supportive community responses, including counseling services, public memorials, and collective mourning rituals, can foster resilience and promote healing. Cultural factors, such as religious beliefs and communal values, play a significant role in shaping how individuals and communities interpret and respond to trauma. In some cultures, communal solidarity and spiritual beliefs provide a robust framework for coping with trauma, while in others, stigma associated with mental health issues may hinder victims from seeking help.

The long-term psychological effects of terrorism are profound and multifaceted. Beyond PTSD and other anxiety disorders, victims may experience chronic depression, substance abuse, and a diminished sense of safety and trust. The pervasive sense of fear and insecurity can alter an individual's worldview, leading to heightened vigilance, mistrust of others, and a pervasive sense of helplessness. These changes can affect personal relationships, career aspirations, and overall life satisfaction. Children and adolescents, in particular, are vulnerable to long-term psychological effects, which can impede their developmental trajectory and lead to enduring emotional and behavioral problems.

Coping mechanisms are crucial in mitigating the psychological trauma of terrorism. Individuals and communities employ a variety of strategies to manage distress and promote healing. Social support, both formal and informal, is a cornerstone of effective coping. Friends, family, and community networks provide emotional support, practical assistance, and a sense of belonging, which are vital for recovery. Professional mental health services, including counseling and therapy, play a critical role in addressing severe psychological conditions. Cognitive-behavioral therapy (CBT), for instance, has been shown to be effective in treating PTSD by helping individuals reframe negative thoughts and develop healthy coping strategies.

In addition to formal interventions, self-help strategies and community-based initiatives are essential for long-term recovery. Mindfulness practices, such as meditation and yoga, can help individuals manage stress and anxiety. Engaging in meaningful activities, such as volunteering or advocacy work, can provide a sense of purpose and agency, aiding in the recovery process. Community-based programs that promote social cohesion and collective healing, such as support groups and commemorative events, foster a shared sense of resilience and solidarity.

The psychological trauma of terrorism also has implications for public policy and mental health services. Governments and health organizations must recognize the need for comprehensive mental health support in the aftermath of terrorist attacks. This includes providing accessible and culturally sensitive mental health services, training healthcare providers in trauma-informed care, and integrating mental health support into emergency response plans. Public awareness campaigns can reduce stigma associated with mental health issues and encourage individuals to seek help. Policy measures that address the broader social determinants of mental health, such as economic stability and social inclusion, are also crucial in building resilient communities capable of withstanding and recovering from terrorist attacks. Understanding the psychological impact of terrorism requires a holistic approach that considers the immediate and long-term effects, individual and societal factors, and the coping mechanisms employed by individuals and communities. By addressing the psychological needs of terrorism victims through comprehensive mental health support, social interventions, and policy measures, society can promote healing and resilience in the face of terrorism's devastating impact.

The coping mechanisms of terrorism victims

Another critical coping mechanism is the engagement in meaningful activities. Terrorism victims often find solace in activities that provide a sense of purpose and normalcy. This can include returning to work, participating in community events, or engaging in hobbies and interests. Such activities can help distract from the traumatic memories and provide a sense of control and predictability in their lives. Additionally, these activities can foster a sense of accomplishment and self-worth, which are essential for psychological recovery. Empowerment through productive engagement can significantly aid in the healing process, helping victims to rebuild their lives and regain a sense of normalcy.

Cognitive-behavioral therapy (CBT) is another effective coping mechanism employed by terrorism victims. This therapeutic approach helps individuals to identify and challenge negative thought patterns and behaviors that may have developed as a result of the trauma. CBT assists victims in reframing their experiences and developing healthier cognitive and emotional responses. Techniques such as exposure therapy, where victims gradually confront and process traumatic memories in a controlled environment, can be particularly effective. By systematically desensitizing themselves to the traumatic event, victims can reduce the intensity of their emotional responses and gain better control over their thoughts and feelings.

Mindfulness and relaxation techniques also play a vital role in the coping mechanisms of terrorism victims. Practices such as meditation, deep breathing exercises, and yoga can help individuals manage stress and anxiety. These techniques promote a state of calm and relaxation, which can be particularly beneficial for those experiencing hyperarousal or intrusive thoughts related to the trauma. Mindfulness encourages victims to stay present and focused on the current moment, reducing the impact of past traumatic events on their current mental state. Regular practice of these techniques can lead to improved emotional regulation and a greater sense of inner peace.

The use of creative arts as a coping mechanism is also noteworthy. Art therapy, music therapy, and other creative outlets provide victims with a non-verbal means of expressing their emotions and processing their experiences. Engaging in creative activities can be both therapeutic and empowering, allowing individuals to communicate feelings that may be difficult to express through words alone. Artistic expression can facilitate emotional release and provide a sense of accomplishment and self-discovery. the act of creating can serve as a distraction from distressing thoughts and memories, offering a respite from the emotional burden of the trauma.

Religious and spiritual practices are often integral to the coping mechanisms of terrorism victims. Many individuals find comfort and strength in their faith, turning to religious rituals, prayer, and spiritual communities for support. These practices can provide a sense of hope, purpose, and connection to a higher power, which can be incredibly reassuring during times of crisis. Spiritual beliefs can offer a framework for understanding and making sense of the trauma, helping victims to find meaning and acceptance in their experiences. Additionally, spiritual communities can offer a supportive environment where victims feel understood and cared for, enhancing their overall well-being.

Physical activity and exercise are also important coping mechanisms for terrorism victims. Regular physical exercise can help reduce symptoms of anxiety and depression, improve mood, and enhance overall physical health. Exercise releases endorphins, which are natural mood lifters, and can provide a healthy outlet for stress and frustration. Activities such as walking, running, swimming, or participating in sports can also promote a sense of normalcy and routine, which is crucial for psychological recovery. Furthermore, physical activity can foster social interaction and community engagement, further supporting the healing process.

Education and learning about trauma and its effects can empower terrorism victims by providing them with knowledge and understanding of their experiences. Educational programs and workshops that focus on trauma, coping strategies, and resilience can equip individuals with the tools they need to manage their symptoms and move forward. Understanding the psychological impact of terrorism and learning about effective coping mechanisms can reduce feelings of helplessness and provide a sense of control. This knowledge can also help victims to recognize and seek appropriate professional help when needed.

Professional support, including counseling and psychotherapy, is a critical resource for terrorism victims. Mental health professionals can provide specialized interventions tailored to the unique needs of each individual. Therapists can help victims process their traumatic experiences, develop coping strategies, and work through any associated mental health issues such as PTSD, depression, or anxiety. The therapeutic relationship itself can be a source of support and validation, providing a safe space for victims to explore their emotions and experiences. Consistent professional support is essential for long-term recovery and resilience.

The role of resilience in coping with terrorism cannot be overstated. Resilience refers to the ability to adapt and recover from adversity, and it plays a significant role in how individuals respond to traumatic events. Some victims naturally possess high levels of resilience, which can aid in their recovery process. However, resilience can also be cultivated through various means such as building strong social networks, developing effective coping strategies, and fostering a positive outlook on life. Programs that focus on enhancing resilience can be particularly beneficial for terrorism victims, providing them with the skills and mindset needed to overcome challenges and thrive despite their experiences.

Engaging in advocacy and activism can also serve as a coping mechanism for terrorism victims. Many individuals find a sense of purpose and empowerment by becoming involved in efforts to prevent future acts of terrorism and support other victims. Advocacy can provide a platform for victims to share their stories, raise awareness, and influence change. This active involvement can foster a sense of agency and control, helping victims to channel their experiences into positive action. Additionally, connecting with others who share similar goals can provide a supportive community and reinforce a sense of solidarity and purpose.

Journaling and expressive writing are valuable coping mechanisms for terrorism victims. Writing about their experiences and emotions can help individuals process and make sense of their trauma. Journaling provides a private space for victims to explore their thoughts and feelings without fear of judgment. This practice can lead to greater self-awareness and emotional clarity, aiding in the healing process. Expressive writing has been shown to have numerous psychological benefits, including reduced stress, improved mood, and enhanced immune function. By regularly engaging in this activity, victims can gain a deeper understanding of their experiences and develop more effective coping strategies.

The establishment of routines and structure is another important coping mechanism for terrorism victims. Establishing a predictable daily routine can provide a sense of stability and control, which is often disrupted by traumatic events. Routines can help victims manage their time and energy, reducing feelings of chaos and uncertainty. Simple activities such as maintaining regular mealtimes, exercise routines, and sleep schedules can significantly impact overall well-being. Structure and predictability can help victims feel more grounded and secure, facilitating their recovery and adjustment to life after trauma.

Humor and laughter, although seemingly incongruous with the gravity of terrorism, can also serve as effective coping mechanisms. Humor can provide a temporary respite from the pain and stress of trauma, offering moments of levity and joy. Laughter releases endorphins and can improve mood, reduce stress, and foster a sense of connection with others. While it is important to approach humor with sensitivity and respect for the seriousness of the trauma, incorporating lightheartedness and positivity into their lives can help victims maintain a balanced perspective and enhance their emotional resilience. Social support, engagement in meaningful activities, cognitive-behavioral therapy, mindfulness practices, creative arts, religious and spiritual beliefs, physical activity, education, professional support, resilience-building, advocacy,

65

journaling, routines, and humor all play crucial roles in helping victims navigate their experiences and rebuild their lives. Understanding and supporting these coping mechanisms is essential for developing effective interventions and fostering resilience in the face of terrorism. By acknowledging and addressing the psychological needs of terrorism victims, we can contribute to their healing and empower them to move forward with hope and strength.

The long-term effects of terrorism

One of the most pervasive long-term effects of terrorism is the development of Post-Traumatic Stress Disorder (PTSD). PTSD is a severe anxiety disorder that arises following exposure to traumatic events, characterized by symptoms such as flashbacks, nightmares, and severe anxiety, as well as uncontrollable thoughts about the event. Victims of terrorism often find themselves reliving the harrowing experiences, which can lead to chronic hyperarousal and hypervigilance. This state of constant alertness disrupts daily functioning and impairs the ability to maintain healthy social relationships. Over time, the persistent stress can lead to physical health problems, including cardiovascular diseases and weakened immune systems, further complicating the recovery process.

Beyond PTSD, the psychological aftermath of terrorism frequently includes depression and anxiety disorders. The overwhelming sense of loss, whether of loved ones, security, or a sense of normalcy, can precipitate profound feelings of hopelessness and despair. These feelings are often compounded by the disruption of community and social networks, which are crucial for emotional support and recovery. The isolation that frequently follows terrorist attacks exacerbates these mental health issues, leading to a vicious cycle of withdrawal and deepening depression. Anxiety disorders, including generalized anxiety disorder and panic disorder, also become prevalent as individuals struggle with an intensified fear of future attacks and an overarching sense of vulnerability.

Children and adolescents are particularly vulnerable to the long-term psychological effects of terrorism. The developmental stages of young individuals are sensitive to environmental stressors, and exposure to violence and terror can hinder normal psychological growth. Children may exhibit regressive behaviors, such as bedwetting or clinginess, and older children and adolescents might develop behavioral problems, including aggression and defiance. The impact on academic performance is also notable, with affected children showing a decline in school engagement and achievement. The long-term educational and social consequences of such disruptions can limit future opportunities and perpetuate cycles of poverty and marginalization.

The psychological effects of terrorism also extend to collective identity and social cohesion. Communities that experience terrorist attacks often undergo significant social fragmentation. Trust among community members can erode, and a pervasive atmosphere of suspicion and fear can replace the sense of solidarity. This breakdown in social cohesion hampers collective resilience and impedes communal recovery efforts. In some cases, the fear and distrust can lead to the stigmatization and marginalization of specific groups, particularly if the terrorist acts are attributed to particular ethnic or religious communities. This dynamic can fuel further social division and conflict, undermining efforts to build inclusive and resilient societies.

Economic impacts are another critical dimension of the long-term effects of terrorism. The mental health burden resulting from terrorism translates into substantial economic costs, including lost productivity, increased healthcare expenditures, and the need for extensive mental health services. Individuals suffering from psychological disorders may find it challenging to maintain employment, leading to financial instability and further exacerbating their mental health struggles. Additionally, the economic strain on healthcare systems to provide adequate mental health support can divert resources from other essential services, creating a ripple effect of economic and social challenges.

the long-term psychological effects of terrorism can influence political attitudes and behaviors. Victims and communities may develop heightened levels of political cynicism and distrust towards government and authority figures, perceiving them as incapable of providing security and protection. This disillusionment can lead to increased support for extremist ideologies and groups, creating a feedback loop that perpetuates the cycle of violence and terrorism. The politicization of trauma and the exploitation of victims' experiences by various political actors can further deepen societal divisions and hinder the development of effective, inclusive policies for addressing terrorism and its aftermath.

Cultural and religious beliefs play a significant role in shaping the psychological responses to terrorism. For many individuals, faith and cultural practices provide a source of resilience and coping mechanisms. However, terrorism can also challenge and disrupt these belief systems, leading to a crisis of faith and identity. The manipulation of religious and cultural narratives by terrorist groups to justify their actions can create confusion and conflict within communities, particularly among youth who may struggle to reconcile these narratives with their personal experiences and values. This cultural dissonance can contribute to identity crises and a sense of alienation, further complicating the psychological recovery process.

The role of media in shaping the psychological impact of terrorism cannot be understated. Media coverage of terrorist attacks often amplifies the sense of fear and insecurity, particularly when it is sensationalized or focuses disproportionately on the perpetrators. This type of coverage can lead to vicarious traumatization, where individuals who were not directly affected by the attacks nonetheless experience significant psychological distress. The continuous exposure to graphic images and reports of terrorism can normalize violence and desensitize individuals to its impact, potentially leading to a culture of fear and paranoia. Media literacy and responsible reporting are crucial in mitigating these effects and promoting a balanced understanding of terrorism and its consequences. The development of PTSD, depression, and anxiety disorders, the impact on children and adolescents, the erosion of social cohesion, economic burdens, and the influence on political attitudes all underscore the pervasive nature of these effects. Addressing these challenges requires a comprehensive approach that includes mental health support, community resilience building, media responsibility, and policies that foster social inclusion and economic stability. Understanding the psychological dimensions of terrorism is essential for developing strategies that not only address immediate security concerns but also promote long-term healing and resilience for individuals and communities affected by terrorism.

Chapter 7: The Media and Terrorism

The role of the media in terrorism

The concept of "terrorism" itself is inherently tied to media coverage. Terrorism, by definition, is a form of violence designed to create an atmosphere of fear and anxiety among a wide audience, far beyond the immediate victims. The media's extensive coverage of terrorist acts fulfills this objective by providing a platform that magnifies the terrorists' reach and influence. When a terrorist attack occurs, the ensuing media frenzy ensures that the incident is broadcasted globally, often in real-time. This immediate and widespread dissemination of information not only heightens public fear but also grants terrorists the publicity they crave, thereby achieving one of their primary goals.

the media's role in framing terrorist events significantly influences public perception and policy responses. The manner in which news outlets report on terrorism—whether they emphasize the ideological motivations behind attacks, the human toll, or the governmental response—shapes how society understands and reacts to these events. Sensationalist reporting, for example, can provoke heightened anxiety and anger, potentially leading to overreactions or the implementation of draconian measures that may infringe on civil liberties. Conversely, balanced and informative reporting can foster a more nuanced understanding of terrorism, promoting public resilience and informed policy decisions.

The symbiotic relationship between terrorism and the media is further complicated by the advent of digital media and social networking platforms. Traditional media outlets are no longer the sole gatekeepers of information. The proliferation of online platforms has democratized information dissemination, enabling terrorist groups to bypass conventional media channels and communicate directly with their target audiences. This shift has empowered terrorist organizations to craft and control their narratives with unprecedented precision and reach. The rise of citizen journalism and user-generated content also means that information about terrorist activities can spread rapidly and widely, often without the filters of professional journalism.

Social media, in particular, has become a critical battleground in the fight against terrorism. Platforms like Twitter, Facebook, and YouTube have been exploited by terrorist groups for recruitment, propaganda, and operational coordination. The viral nature of social media content means that a single post can reach millions of people within hours, creating a ripple effect that amplifies the psychological impact of terrorist activities. Counterterrorism efforts, therefore, must increasingly incorporate strategies to monitor and mitigate the use of social media by terrorist entities. This includes developing sophisticated algorithms to detect and remove extremist content, as well as collaborating with tech companies to enhance digital literacy and counter-messaging initiatives.

The influence of media on terrorism is not solely negative. While it is undeniable that media coverage can inadvertently aid terrorist objectives, responsible journalism can also play a crucial role in counterterrorism efforts. By providing accurate, timely, and contextual information, the media can help demystify terrorism, reduce public panic, and foster a more informed and resilient society. Investigative reporting that exposes the underlying causes of terrorism, such as socio-political grievances and ideological radicalization, can contribute to long-term solutions by addressing the root problems rather than merely reacting to symptoms.

Furthermore, the media's role in holding governments accountable is vital in ensuring that counterterrorism measures are both effective and respectful of human rights. Comprehensive coverage of governmental actions, including military operations, legislative changes, and intelligence activities, ensures transparency and helps prevent abuses of power. This watchdog function of the media is essential in maintaining the balance between security and liberty, ensuring that the fight against terrorism does not come at the expense of democratic values and civil liberties.

The ethical considerations surrounding media coverage of terrorism are profound and multifaceted. Journalists and media organizations face the challenging task of reporting on terrorism in a way that informs the public without unduly amplifying the terrorists' message. This delicate balance requires a commitment to ethical journalism principles, including accuracy, fairness, and sensitivity. The media must navigate the fine line between providing comprehensive coverage and avoiding the sensationalism that can play into the hands of terrorists. This ethical tightrope is particularly challenging in the context of live reporting, where the pressure to deliver real-time updates can lead to the dissemination of unverified or incomplete information.

The psychological impact of media coverage on the public is another critical aspect of the media-terrorism nexus. The constant exposure to graphic images and reports of terrorist attacks can lead to heightened levels of anxiety, stress, and fear among the population. This phenomenon, known as "mean world syndrome," suggests that extensive media coverage of violence and terrorism can distort public perception, making the world seem more dangerous than it actually is. This distorted perception can have significant societal implications, including increased support for stringent security measures, heightened prejudice against certain groups, and a general erosion of trust in public institutions.

The role of media literacy in mitigating the negative effects of terrorism coverage cannot be overstated. Educating the public about how to critically evaluate media content, understand the motivations behind terrorist propaganda, and recognize the difference between sensationalism and responsible reporting is essential. Media literacy programs can empower individuals to consume news more discerningly, reducing the psychological impact of terrorism coverage and fostering a more informed and resilient society. While the media can inadvertently amplify the impact of terrorist activities, it also has the potential to play a constructive role in counterterrorism efforts. By adhering to ethical journalism standards, promoting media literacy, and leveraging digital platforms responsibly, the media can help mitigate the fear and anxiety generated by terrorism. Ultimately, the goal should be to strike a balance between informing the public and preventing the undue glorification of terrorist acts, ensuring that the media remains a force for enlightenment rather than exploitation in the context of terrorism.

The ethical considerations of reporting on terrorism

One primary ethical concern is the potential for media coverage to amplify the effects of terrorism. Terrorist acts are often meticulously planned to attract maximum publicity, turning violence into a spectacle that garners widespread attention. When media outlets provide extensive coverage, they inadvertently fulfill the terrorists' objectives by magnifying the impact of their actions. This amplification can inspire further acts of terrorism, as perpetrators seek to replicate the attention and notoriety achieved by previous attacks. Therefore, journalists must carefully consider the extent and nature of their coverage, striving to report on terrorism in a way that informs the public without unnecessarily escalating fear or providing a platform for terrorist propaganda.

Another critical ethical issue is the risk of glorifying terrorists and their actions. Media portrayals that focus extensively on the personal backgrounds, motivations, and ideologies of terrorists can inadvertently elevate them to a status of anti-heroes or martyrs in the eyes of some individuals. This kind of coverage can romanticize terrorism, making it appear as a viable avenue for those seeking to express their grievances or achieve recognition. Ethical reporting should therefore avoid undue emphasis on the personal details of terrorists, focusing instead on the broader context, the victims, and the societal impacts of the attacks. By humanizing the victims and highlighting the resilience of communities, the media can shift the narrative away from the terrorists and towards the collective response to such acts.

The accuracy and reliability of information are also paramount in ethical reporting on terrorism. In the immediate aftermath of a terrorist attack, the rush to break news can lead to the dissemination of unverified or incorrect information. This not only undermines the credibility of the media but can also exacerbate public fear and confusion. Ethical journalists must prioritize verification and fact-checking, even if it means delaying the release of information. Transparent communication about what is known and what is still under investigation helps build trust with the audience and prevents the spread of misinformation.

Furthermore, the media must navigate the fine line between informing the public and respecting the privacy and dignity of victims and their families. Intrusive reporting that delves into the personal lives of victims or broadcasts graphic images of the aftermath can cause additional trauma and suffering. Ethical considerations demand that journalists exercise restraint and sensitivity, ensuring that their reporting does not contribute to the distress of those affected by terrorism. This involves making careful editorial decisions about what images and details are necessary to convey the story without causing harm.

The language and terminology used in reporting on terrorism also carry significant ethical implications. The words chosen to describe terrorists and their actions can influence public perception and policy. Terms like "terrorist" versus "militant" or "freedom fighter" are not just semantic differences; they carry distinct connotations that shape how audiences understand and respond to the events being reported. Ethical journalism requires careful consideration of language to avoid biased or inflammatory rhetoric that could exacerbate tensions or reinforce stereotypes. Objective and neutral language helps ensure that reporting remains fair and balanced, contributing to a more informed and reasoned public discourse.

The role of the media in counterterrorism efforts presents another ethical dilemma. While journalists have a responsibility to hold authorities accountable and scrutinize counterterrorism policies, they must also avoid becoming tools of government propaganda. Ethical reporting involves a commitment to independence and critical analysis, questioning the effectiveness and implications of counterterrorism measures. This includes examining potential human rights abuses, the impact on civil liberties, and the broader social and political consequences of security policies. By providing a balanced and critical perspective, the media can contribute to a more nuanced and informed public debate on how best to address the threat of terrorism.

Ethical considerations also extend to the use of social media and digital platforms in reporting on terrorism. The rapid dissemination of information through these channels can both aid and hinder responsible journalism. On one hand, social media provides a platform for real-time updates and diverse perspectives, allowing the media to reach a wider audience quickly. On the other hand, the lack of editorial oversight and the potential for misinformation to spread rapidly pose significant ethical challenges. Journalists must exercise caution in using social media sources, verifying the authenticity of information before sharing it with the public. Additionally, they should be mindful of the echo chamber effect, where sensational or biased content can be amplified within closed networks, further polarizing public opinion.

the ethical considerations of reporting on terrorism intersect with issues of national security and freedom of the press. Governments often seek to control the flow of information related to terrorism, citing national security concerns. Ethical journalism requires navigating this tension, advocating for transparency and the public's right to know while recognizing legitimate security needs. This involves engaging in a constructive dialogue with authorities, pushing for access to information without compromising national security. Journalists must also be vigilant against attempts by governments to manipulate the media for propaganda purposes, maintaining their role as independent watchdogs.

In addition to these broader ethical considerations, the media must also consider the impact of their reporting on societal cohesion and intergroup relations. Terrorism often seeks to exploit divisions within society, fostering fear and mistrust between different communities. Ethical reporting can play a crucial role in countering this by promoting understanding and solidarity. This involves highlighting stories of resilience, cooperation, and unity in the face of terror, as well as addressing the root causes of radicalization and extremism. By providing a platform for diverse voices and perspectives, the media can help build a more inclusive and resilient society. Journalists must strike a delicate balance between informing the public and avoiding the amplification of terrorist objectives. This involves careful consideration of the potential impact of their coverage, a commitment to accuracy and sensitivity, and a critical approach to both terrorism and counterterrorism measures. Ethical journalism in this context is not just about reporting facts; it is about shaping a narrative that fosters understanding, resilience, and informed public discourse. Through responsible and ethical reporting, the media can play a crucial role in mitigating the effects of terrorism and promoting a more just and peaceful society.

The impact of terrorism on the media

The media's coverage of terrorism often oscillates between responsible reporting and sensationalism. Responsible journalism aims to inform the public accurately and objectively, providing context and analysis to foster understanding and critical thinking. Sensationalism, on the other hand, prioritizes dramatic and emotionally charged narratives that capture audience attention and drive ratings. This latter approach can inadvertently amplify the terrorists' message, spreading fear and anxiety among the populace. The balance between these two approaches is delicate and often influenced by commercial pressures, editorial policies, and the immediacy of news cycles.

One of the primary ways terrorism impacts the media is through agenda-setting. By their very nature, terrorist acts are designed to disrupt normalcy and draw attention. The media, in covering these events extensively, places terrorism at the forefront of public consciousness. This heightened visibility not only amplifies the perceived threat but also influences public opinion and policy-making. The repeated exposure to terrorist acts through the media can create a climate of fear and insecurity, prompting calls for stricter security measures and potentially leading to the erosion of civil liberties.

The psychological impact of terrorism on the media and its audience is profound. Media consumers are subjected to a barrage of images and reports that can induce stress and trauma. The constant portrayal of violence and destruction can desensitize individuals, making them more accepting of extreme measures to combat terrorism. This desensitization can also lead to a skewed perception of risk, where the fear of terrorism outweighs the actual statistical likelihood of being affected by it. The media's role in shaping these perceptions is crucial, as it can either contribute to a balanced understanding of risks or exacerbate unfounded fears.

The media's portrayal of terrorists and their motives also plays a significant role in shaping public perception. By framing terrorists as either freedom fighters or deranged criminals, the media influences how society views and responds to terrorism. This framing can either legitimize or delegitimize the terrorists' cause, impacting international support and domestic policy. The language used in media reports, the selection of images, and the overall narrative tone all contribute to this framing process. It is essential for journalists to be mindful of these choices to avoid inadvertently promoting terrorist agendas.

The advent of digital media and social networks has further complicated the relationship between terrorism and the media. Traditional media outlets are no longer the sole gatekeepers of information. Terrorist organizations have increasingly turned to the internet to disseminate their propaganda, recruit members, and coordinate activities. Social media platforms, with their vast reach and immediacy, have become fertile ground for terrorist messaging. The viral nature of online content means that terrorist acts can quickly gain global attention, amplifying their impact and reach. The challenge for the media and policymakers is to address this new landscape without infringing on freedom of speech and digital rights.

The ethical considerations surrounding media coverage of terrorism are paramount. Journalists and editors must navigate the fine line between informing the public and avoiding the glorification of terrorists. Ethical reporting involves careful consideration of the potential consequences of media content. This includes avoiding the publication of graphic images that could traumatize viewers or inspire copycat attacks, and ensuring that terrorist acts are not depicted in a way that could be seen as heroic or justified. The responsibility to report truthfully and responsibly is a cornerstone of ethical journalism, particularly in the context of terrorism where the stakes are exceptionally high.

The impact of media coverage on terrorism's recruitment efforts cannot be understated. Terrorist organizations often rely on media exposure to attract new members and sympathizers. The portrayal of terrorists as powerful and influential figures can appeal to individuals seeking a sense of belonging or purpose. The media's role in either countering or reinforcing these narratives is critical. By providing a nuanced and balanced perspective, the media can help undermine terrorist recruitment efforts. Highlighting the stories of de-radicalized individuals and showcasing the negative consequences of terrorism can serve as powerful counter-narratives.

The media's influence extends to the realm of policy-making and international relations. Public opinion, shaped by media coverage, can drive political agendas and influence government responses to terrorism. The media's portrayal of terrorist incidents can affect diplomatic relations, military strategies, and legislative measures. In this regard, the media serves as a powerful intermediary between the public and policymakers. Responsible media coverage can foster informed debate and contribute to the development of effective counter-terrorism strategies. Conversely, sensationalist or biased reporting can lead to misguided policies and heightened international tensions.

The role of the media in preventing terrorism is also significant. By promoting awareness and understanding of the root causes of terrorism, the media can contribute to long-term solutions. This involves reporting on social, economic, and political factors that may contribute to radicalization and extremism. The media can also play a role in promoting dialogue and reconciliation between conflicting parties. By providing a platform for diverse voices and perspectives, the media can help bridge divides and foster mutual understanding. This proactive approach to journalism can contribute to a more informed and resilient society capable of resisting extremist ideologies. The media's role in shaping public perception, influencing policy, and either countering or inadvertently aiding terrorist objectives is crucial. Navigating this complex landscape requires a delicate balance between responsible reporting and ethical considerations. As the media landscape continues to evolve with the rise of digital platforms, the challenges and opportunities in this domain will undoubtedly grow. It is imperative for journalists, editors, and media organizations to remain vigilant and committed to the principles of ethical journalism in their coverage of terrorism. Only through such diligence can the media fulfill its vital role in society while mitigating the risks associated with the amplification of terrorist narratives.

Chapter 8: The Politics of Terrorism

The use of terrorism for political purposes

One of the primary themes explored in this one is the strategic rationale behind political terrorism. Terrorist groups often perceive violence as a legitimate means to achieve political ends, especially when conventional political avenues are perceived as ineffective or inaccessible. This perception is rooted in a belief that extreme measures are necessary to bring attention to their cause, provoke a response from the targeted state, and ultimately, to instigate change. The strategic use of terrorism is thus not merely an act of violence but a calculated attempt to communicate a political message, challenge the existing power structures, and mobilize support among sympathizers.

The psychological underpinnings of political terrorism are also critically examined. Terrorists often exhibit a strong sense of grievance and a belief in the righteousness of their cause. This conviction can be so profound that it justifies, in their minds, the use of violence against civilians and non-combatants. The psychological profile of terrorists typically includes a high degree of commitment to their ideological beliefs, a willingness to sacrifice personal well-being for the collective goal, and a propensity for risk-taking behavior. Understanding these psychological traits is essential for comprehending why individuals are drawn to terrorist organizations and how they rationalize their actions.

the one discusses the role of group dynamics and leadership in shaping the use of terrorism for political purposes. Terrorist organizations are often hierarchical, with charismatic leaders who play a crucial role in indoctrinating members and directing operations. These leaders exploit the grievances of their followers, channeling their anger and frustration into violent action. The group provides a sense of identity and belonging, reinforcing the commitment to the cause and the belief that their actions are justified. This collective identity can be a powerful motivator, making individuals more willing to engage in acts of terrorism.

The impact of political terrorism on both the targeted society and the international community is another critical aspect analyzed in this one. Terrorism aims to create fear and uncertainty, undermining public confidence in the government's ability to protect its citizens. This erosion of trust can have significant political ramifications, potentially leading to changes in policy, shifts in public opinion, and even alterations in the balance of power. The response of the targeted state to terrorist acts is also a crucial factor; overly aggressive or repressive measures can exacerbate the situation, fueling further radicalization and recruitment for terrorist groups.

The one also addresses the media's role in the propagation of terrorism for political purposes. Media coverage can amplify the effects of terrorist acts, providing terrorists with a platform to disseminate their message and garner attention. The sensationalism and widespread coverage of terrorist incidents can increase public anxiety and pressure governments to respond, often in ways that align with the terrorists' objectives. This symbiotic relationship between terrorism and media underscores the importance of responsible reporting and the need for strategies to mitigate the sensationalism that can inadvertently support terrorist goals.

Furthermore, the one explores the effectiveness of various counter-terrorism strategies. It highlights the importance of addressing the root causes of terrorism, such as political grievances, social injustices, and economic disparities. Effective counter-terrorism efforts must balance security measures with efforts to address these underlying issues, promoting political inclusion, social equity, and economic development. The one suggests that a comprehensive approach that combines security, political, and socio-economic strategies is essential for mitigating the threat of political terrorism.

In addition, the one examines the international dimensions of political terrorism. Transnational terrorist networks pose significant challenges to national security and international stability. The globalization of terrorism means that terrorist groups can operate across borders, exploiting weak governance, conflict zones, and ungoverned spaces. This necessitates international cooperation and coordination in intelligence sharing, law enforcement, and counter-terrorism strategies. The one emphasizes the need for a unified global approach to combat the transnational nature of modern terrorism.

The ethical and moral considerations of counter-terrorism efforts are also discussed. The use of torture, extrajudicial killings, and other controversial tactics can undermine the moral authority of the state and fuel further radicalization. The one argues for a balanced approach that respects human rights and upholds the rule of law while effectively addressing the threat of terrorism. Ethical counter-terrorism strategies that prioritize human rights can enhance the legitimacy of the state and reduce the appeal of terrorist ideologies.

The one also delves into the role of technology in the use of terrorism for political purposes. Advances in technology have provided terrorist groups with new tools for planning and executing attacks, spreading propaganda, and recruiting members. Social media, in particular, has become a powerful platform for terrorist organizations to disseminate their message, radicalize individuals, and coordinate activities. The one highlights the need for innovative approaches to counter the use of technology by terrorists, including cyber security measures and counter-narratives to challenge extremist ideologies online.

the one considers the future of political terrorism and the evolving nature of the threat. As terrorist tactics and strategies continue to evolve, it is crucial for governments and international bodies to adapt and develop new approaches to counter this threat. The one suggests that a proactive and adaptive strategy, informed by a deep understanding of the psychological and strategic dimensions of terrorism, is essential for effectively addressing the challenges posed by political terrorism. By exploring the strategic, psychological, and social dimensions of political terrorism, the one offers valuable insights into the motivations and tactics of terrorist groups. It underscores the importance of a multifaceted approach to counter-terrorism that addresses the root causes of terrorism, leverages international cooperation, and upholds ethical standards. Understanding the complex interplay of factors that drive political terrorism is essential for developing effective strategies to mitigate this persistent and evolving threat.

The counterterrorism policies of governments

In addition to preventive measures, counterterrorism policies also encompass reactive strategies designed to respond to and mitigate the impact of terrorist attacks. These strategies include emergency response protocols, crisis management frameworks, and public safety initiatives. Governments typically establish specialized units within their security and law enforcement agencies to handle terrorist incidents. These units are trained to act swiftly and decisively to minimize casualties and restore order in the aftermath of an attack. The coordination between various levels of government and between different agencies is crucial for the success of these efforts. Furthermore, international cooperation plays a significant role, as terrorist networks often operate across national borders. Information sharing and joint operations between countries are essential components of global counterterrorism efforts.

A critical aspect of counterterrorism policies is the legal and judicial framework within which they operate. Governments must balance the need for security with the protection of individual rights and freedoms. This balance is often contentious, as stringent counterterrorism laws can sometimes lead to overreach and the erosion of democratic principles. For instance, laws that allow for indefinite detention without trial or extensive surveillance powers can be seen as draconian and detrimental to the rule of law. Therefore, the legislative process surrounding counterterrorism measures is often rigorous, involving debates and revisions to ensure that they are both effective and just. Legal safeguards, such as judicial oversight and periodic reviews of counterterrorism laws, are implemented to prevent abuses of power.

The role of intelligence agencies in counterterrorism cannot be overstated. These agencies are responsible for collecting, analyzing, and disseminating information regarding terrorist activities. They employ a variety of methods, including human intelligence, signals intelligence, and cyber intelligence, to gather data on terrorist organizations and their activities. The analysis of this data helps in identifying patterns and predicting potential threats. However, the secretive nature of intelligence work can sometimes lead to controversies, particularly when intelligence operations involve covert actions or when intelligence failures result in successful terrorist attacks. Transparency and accountability mechanisms are therefore crucial to maintaining public trust and ensuring that intelligence agencies operate within the bounds of the law.

Public perception and communication strategies are integral to the success of counterterrorism policies. Governments must maintain a delicate balance between informing the public about potential threats and avoiding panic or hysteria. Effective communication involves clear, consistent messaging that reassures the public while also providing practical advice on how to stay safe. In the event of a terrorist attack, the way a government communicates with the public can significantly influence public morale and confidence in the authorities. Crisis communication strategies that emphasize resilience and unity can help mitigate the psychological impact of terrorism on society.

Economic considerations also play a significant role in shaping counterterrorism policies. The allocation of resources to counterterrorism efforts must be balanced against other national priorities, such as healthcare, education, and infrastructure. The costs associated with counterterrorism can be substantial, encompassing expenditures on security personnel, technology, and international collaborations. Governments must therefore make strategic decisions about how to allocate limited resources in a way that maximizes security without compromising other essential services. Additionally, the economic impact of terrorist attacks, including damage to infrastructure and loss of business confidence, can have long-term repercussions on a country's economy. Counterterrorism policies that effectively prevent and respond to attacks can help mitigate these economic impacts.

The effectiveness of counterterrorism policies is also influenced by the broader geopolitical context. International relations, diplomatic efforts, and global security dynamics all play a part in shaping how countries approach counterterrorism. For instance, alliances and partnerships with other nations can enhance a country's counterterrorism capabilities through shared intelligence and joint military operations. Conversely, strained international relations can hinder cooperation and make it more difficult to address transnational terrorist threats. The global nature of terrorism necessitates a coordinated international response, with countries working together to address the root causes of terrorism and disrupt terrorist networks.

The psychological dimension of counterterrorism is another critical area of focus. Understanding the motivations and ideologies that drive individuals to engage in terrorism can inform the development of more effective counterterrorism strategies. Psychological profiling and behavioral analysis are used to identify potential terrorists and understand their decision-making processes. This understanding can help in designing interventions that aim to prevent radicalization and de-radicalize individuals who have already been radicalized. Programs that focus on education, community engagement, and counter-narratives to extremist ideologies are essential components of a comprehensive counterterrorism strategy.

Technology and innovation are continually shaping the landscape of counterterrorism. Advances in technology have provided governments with new tools to detect and prevent terrorist activities. These include biometric identification systems, drone surveillance, and artificial intelligence-driven data analysis. However, the rapid pace of technological change also presents challenges, as terrorists can exploit new technologies for their purposes. Governments must therefore stay ahead of the curve by continuously updating their technological capabilities and developing innovative solutions to counter emerging threats. The integration of technology into counterterrorism efforts requires a careful balance between leveraging new tools and safeguarding against potential misuse or overreach.

The ethical considerations surrounding counterterrorism policies are profound and complex. The use of force, surveillance, and detention in the name of counterterrorism raises significant ethical questions. Governments must navigate these dilemmas by adhering to ethical principles and international human rights standards. The principle of proportionality, for example, dictates that the measures taken to combat terrorism should be proportionate to the threat posed. Similarly, the principle of necessity requires that counterterrorism measures should be implemented only when there is a clear and present danger. Ethical oversight bodies and public scrutiny play a crucial role in ensuring that counterterrorism policies do not violate ethical norms.

Counterterrorism policies must also take into account the social and cultural dimensions of terrorism. Terrorism often emerges from complex socio-political contexts, including grievances related to political marginalization, economic inequality, and social injustice. Addressing these underlying issues is essential for preventing the spread of extremist ideologies and reducing the appeal of terrorism. Community-based approaches that foster social cohesion, promote dialogue, and address grievances can be effective in preventing radicalization. Additionally, cultural sensitivity and awareness are important in designing counterterrorism strategies that resonate with diverse populations and avoid stigmatizing specific groups.

The role of education in counterterrorism cannot be overlooked. Educational programs that promote critical thinking, tolerance, and understanding of different cultures and religions can help counter the narratives propagated by terrorist organizations. By fostering an informed and resilient citizenry, governments can reduce the susceptibility of individuals to extremist ideologies. Educational institutions can also play a role in identifying and addressing early signs of radicalization among students. Integrating counterterrorism education into school curricula and promoting research on terrorism and radicalization are important steps in building a society that is better equipped to resist and respond to terrorist threats.

To sum up, the evaluation and adaptation of counterterrorism policies are essential for their long-term success. Governments must regularly assess the effectiveness of their counterterrorism measures and make necessary adjustments based on evolving threats and changing circumstances. This involves continuous monitoring, evaluation, and feedback mechanisms to identify strengths and weaknesses in the current approach. Adapting policies in response to new information and emerging trends ensures that counterterrorism efforts remain relevant and effective in addressing the ever-changing landscape of global terrorism. The dynamic nature of terrorism requires a flexible and responsive approach, with governments continually refining their strategies to stay ahead of the curve. They encompass a wide range of preventive and reactive measures, legal frameworks, intelligence operations, public communication strategies, and ethical considerations. The effectiveness of these policies depends on a balanced approach that safeguards security while protecting individual rights and freedoms. The dynamic and complex nature of terrorism necessitates continuous adaptation and innovation in counterterrorism strategies. By addressing the root causes of terrorism, leveraging technology, and fostering international cooperation, governments can enhance their ability to prevent and respond to terrorist threats. Ultimately, the goal of counterterrorism policies is to create a safer and more secure world for all.

The international cooperation on counterterrorism

One of the cornerstones of international cooperation on counterterrorism is the establishment of global and regional frameworks that facilitate collaboration among states. The United Nations (UN) plays a pivotal role in this regard, providing a platform for member states to develop and implement counterterrorism policies. The UN Global Counter-Terrorism Strategy, adopted in 2006, underscores the importance of international cooperation in addressing the root causes of terrorism, enhancing state capacity to prevent and combat terrorism, and ensuring respect for human rights in counterterrorism efforts. This strategy emphasizes the need for a comprehensive approach that combines security measures with efforts to promote dialogue, understanding, and reconciliation.

Regional organizations also contribute significantly to counterterrorism cooperation. For instance, the European Union (EU) has developed a robust counterterrorism strategy that includes measures to enhance border security, improve information sharing among member states, and support capacity-building initiatives in third countries. Similarly, the African Union (AU) has established the African Centre for the Study and Research on Terrorism (ACSRT) to coordinate regional efforts and facilitate the exchange of information and best practices among member states. These regional frameworks are crucial for addressing the specific challenges and contexts of different regions, thereby tailoring counterterrorism measures to be more effective and contextually relevant.

Intelligence sharing is another critical component of international counterterrorism cooperation. Given the transnational nature of terrorist networks, timely and accurate intelligence is essential for preempting attacks and dismantling terrorist infrastructures. The establishment of intelligence-sharing networks, such as the Counterterrorism Intelligence Sharing (CTIS) framework, allows countries to exchange information on terrorist threats, movements, and activities. This collaborative approach enhances situational awareness and enables states to take proactive measures to disrupt terrorist plots. Furthermore, international intelligence-sharing agreements, such as the Five Eyes alliance among the United States, the United Kingdom, Canada, Australia, and New Zealand, exemplify the depth of cooperation required to address sophisticated and well-organized terrorist networks.

Legal frameworks are also integral to international counterterrorism cooperation. International treaties and conventions, such as the International Convention for the Suppression of the Financing of Terrorism and the Convention on the Prevention and Punishment of Crimes against Internationally Protected Persons, provide a legal basis for cooperation in combating terrorism. These treaties oblige signatory states to criminalize various acts of terrorism, enhance their legal systems to facilitate extradition and mutual legal assistance, and cooperate in investigating and prosecuting terrorism-related offenses. By adhering to these legal instruments, states demonstrate their commitment to a unified global front against terrorism, ensuring that terrorists are denied safe havens and are brought to justice.

Operational cooperation in counterterrorism often involves joint military and law enforcement operations. Multinational coalitions, such as the Global Coalition to Defeat ISIS, exemplify the collaborative efforts required to combat large-scale terrorist organizations. These coalitions bring together the military, intelligence, and law enforcement capabilities of multiple nations to conduct operations against terrorist groups, secure liberated territories, and support stabilization efforts. The success of such coalitions depends on the willingness of member states to contribute resources, share intelligence, and coordinate their actions effectively. Joint operations not only degrade terrorist capabilities but also demonstrate the international community's resolve to confront and defeat terrorism.

Capacity-building initiatives are essential for enhancing the ability of states, particularly in developing regions, to combat terrorism effectively. These initiatives often involve training and equipping local security forces, strengthening legal and regulatory frameworks, and promoting good governance and human rights. International organizations, such as the United Nations Office of Counter-Terrorism (UNOCT) and the Global Counterterrorism Forum (GCTF), play a crucial role in providing technical assistance and facilitating capacity-building programs. By enhancing the capabilities of national and regional actors, these initiatives contribute to the sustainability of counterterrorism efforts and ensure that states are better prepared to address the evolving threats posed by terrorism.

The role of international financial institutions in counterterrorism cooperation cannot be overlooked. Terrorism financing is a critical aspect of counterterrorism efforts, as terrorist organizations rely on financial resources to sustain their operations. International cooperation in this area involves tracking and disrupting financial flows, implementing stringent regulatory measures, and enhancing the transparency of financial systems. Institutions such as the Financial Action Task Force (FATF) set international standards and promote effective implementation of legal, regulatory, and operational measures to combat money laundering and terrorism financing. Cooperation in this domain is crucial for ensuring that terrorist organizations are deprived of the financial means to carry out their activities.

Public diplomacy and counter-messaging efforts are also vital components of international cooperation on counterterrorism. Terrorist organizations often exploit ideological narratives to recruit and radicalize individuals, making it essential to counter these narratives with alternative messages that promote peace, tolerance, and understanding. Public diplomacy initiatives, such as the Strong Cities Network, bring together local governments, civil society organizations, and other stakeholders to share best practices and develop strategies for countering violent extremism at the community level. By fostering dialogue and promoting inclusive narratives, these efforts help to undermine the appeal of terrorist ideologies and prevent radicalization.

Challenges to international cooperation on counterterrorism are numerous and complex. Differences in national priorities, legal systems, and political agendas can hinder effective collaboration. the proliferation of non-state actors and the emergence of new technologies, such as the internet and social media, present new challenges for counterterrorism efforts. Addressing these challenges requires a flexible and adaptive approach that takes into account the evolving nature of terrorism and the diverse contexts in which it manifests. By establishing global and regional frameworks, enhancing intelligence sharing, developing legal instruments, conducting joint operations, building capacities, and engaging in public diplomacy, the international community can effectively address the complex and evolving threat of terrorism. While challenges remain, continued commitment to cooperation and collaboration is essential for ensuring global security and stability.

Chapter 9: The Future of Terrorism

The trends in terrorism

Another notable trend is the growing use of cyberterrorism. As society becomes increasingly reliant on digital infrastructure, the potential for cyber-attacks to cause widespread disruption and fear has grown exponentially. Terrorists are no longer confined to physical acts of violence; they can now target critical infrastructure, financial systems, and communication networks from remote locations. This shift not only expands the reach of terrorism but also introduces a new dimension of psychological warfare, where the threat of an attack can be as impactful as the attack itself. The potential for cyberterrorism to cripple essential services and sow widespread panic makes it a particularly insidious threat in the modern age.

The role of ideology in terrorism is also evolving. While religious extremism, particularly jihadist ideology, has dominated the terrorism landscape for the past few decades, there is a noticeable resurgence of far-right and white supremacist terrorism. This shift is partly driven by socio-political factors, including economic instability, immigration, and cultural changes. Far-right terrorists often exploit online platforms to spread their ideologies and recruit members, creating echo chambers that reinforce their beliefs and incite violence. The rise of far-right terrorism underscores the need for a nuanced understanding of the diverse ideological motivations behind terrorist acts and the necessity of tailored counterterrorism strategies to address these varied threats.

Technological advancements also play a dual role in shaping the future of terrorism. On one hand, technology offers terrorists new tools and methods to carry out attacks, such as drones, 3D printing, and bioweapons. These technologies lower the barriers to entry for conducting sophisticated attacks and increase the potential for mass casualties and destruction. On the other hand, technology also provides counterterrorism agencies with advanced tools for surveillance, intelligence gathering, and disruption of terrorist networks. The challenge lies in balancing the benefits of technological innovation with the need to protect privacy and civil liberties, ensuring that counterterrorism measures do not inadvertently erode the very freedoms they aim to protect.

Globalization continues to influence the dynamics of terrorism. The interconnectedness of the modern world facilitates the spread of terrorist ideologies and the movement of terrorists across borders. This globalization of terrorism is evident in the increasing number of transnational terrorist networks that operate across multiple countries and regions. These networks often exploit weak governance and conflict zones to establish safe havens and training grounds. The global nature of terrorism necessitates international cooperation and coordination in counterterrorism efforts, as no single country can effectively combat terrorism in isolation. The sharing of intelligence, joint operations, and harmonization of legal frameworks are essential components of a robust global response to terrorism.

The psychological aspect of terrorism remains a critical area of study. Understanding the motivations and psychological profiles of terrorists can provide valuable insights into their behavior and decision-making processes. Research indicates that terrorists are often driven by a complex interplay of personal, ideological, and situational factors. For instance, feelings of alienation, perceived injustice, and the desire for significance can contribute to radicalization. By addressing these underlying issues through social policies, community engagement, and counter-narratives, societies can potentially reduce the appeal of terrorist ideologies and prevent radicalization.

The impact of media and communication technologies on terrorism cannot be overstated. The proliferation of social media and instant communication platforms has transformed how terrorist organizations propagate their messages and recruit members. These technologies enable terrorists to reach a global audience, spread propaganda, and incite violence with unprecedented speed and scale. The media's role in shaping public perception and government responses to terrorism is also significant. Responsible reporting and counternarratives can mitigate the sensationalism often associated with terrorist acts, reducing their impact and preventing the spread of fear and panic.

The future of terrorism is also likely to be influenced by environmental and climate changes. Climate change can exacerbate existing social, economic, and political tensions, creating fertile ground for terrorist recruitment and radicalization. Environmental degradation, natural disasters, and resource scarcity can lead to mass displacements, conflicts, and the weakening of state control, which terrorist groups can exploit to further their agendas. Addressing the root causes of environmental instability and promoting sustainable development are crucial for mitigating these risks and preventing the emergence of new terrorist threats.

The evolution of terrorist financing methods is another critical trend. Traditional sources of funding, such as state sponsorship, criminal activities, and donations, remain significant. However, the rise of cryptocurrencies and online fundraising platforms has provided terrorists with new avenues for raising and transferring funds. These digital financial tools offer a degree of anonymity and security that traditional methods do not, making it more challenging for authorities to trace and disrupt terrorist financing networks. Effective counterterrorism strategies must adapt to these new financial technologies, implementing robust regulatory frameworks and international cooperation to curb terrorist financing.

The increasing use of artificial intelligence (AI) and machine learning in counterterrorism efforts represents a promising development. AI can enhance the ability to detect and predict terrorist activities by analyzing vast amounts of data, identifying patterns, and generating actionable intelligence. Machine learning algorithms can sift through social media, communications, and financial transactions to identify potential threats and prevent attacks before they occur. However, the use of AI in counterterrorism also raises ethical and legal concerns, particularly regarding privacy, bias, and the potential for misuse. Ensuring that AI technologies are developed and deployed responsibly is essential for maintaining public trust and upholding human rights.

The role of education and community engagement in preventing terrorism is increasingly recognized as a vital component of a comprehensive counterterrorism strategy. Education programs that promote critical thinking, tolerance, and understanding can help inoculate young people against extremist ideologies. Community engagement initiatives that foster dialogue, inclusion, and social cohesion can address the underlying grievances that contribute to radicalization. By building resilient communities and empowering individuals to reject violence, societies can create a more robust defense against the spread of terrorism. The decentralization of terrorist organizations, the rise of cyberterrorism, the evolving role of ideology, technological advancements, globalization, psychological factors, media influence, environmental changes, terrorist financing, and the use of AI all contribute to the complex landscape of modern terrorism. Effective counterterrorism strategies must be adaptable, multifaceted, and collaborative, addressing both the immediate threats and the underlying drivers of terrorism. By understanding these trends and their implications, policymakers, practitioners, and researchers can develop more informed and effective approaches to preventing and responding to terrorism in the future.

The challenges of preventing terrorism

One of the most significant challenges in preventing terrorism lies in the psychological profiles of terrorists. These individuals are often driven by a potent mix of ideological fervor, personal grievances, and a desire for significance. The one elucidates that understanding these motivations is crucial for developing effective counterterrorism strategies. However, the heterogeneity of terrorist profiles complicates this task. Not all terrorists fit a single mold; they come from diverse backgrounds, possess varying levels of education, and are motivated by a spectrum of ideologies ranging from religious extremism to ethno-nationalist separatism.

This diversity demands a nuanced approach to counterterrorism that goes beyond simplistic profiling and instead focuses on the intricate web of factors that drive individuals towards violence.

Furthermore, the psychological manipulation techniques employed by terrorist organizations are sophisticated and insidious. These groups exploit cognitive biases, social isolation, and existential anxieties to recruit and indoctrinate individuals. They create a sense of belonging and purpose, which can be incredibly compelling to those who feel marginalized or disillusioned with mainstream society. Counterterrorism efforts must, therefore, include strategies to address these psychological vulnerabilities, such as community engagement programs that foster a sense of inclusion and resilience against extremist narratives.

Technological advancements pose another formidable challenge in the fight against terrorism. The digital age has provided terrorists with powerful tools for communication, recruitment, and operational planning. Social media platforms, encrypted messaging apps, and the dark web offer terrorists a means to disseminate propaganda, radicalize individuals, and coordinate attacks with unprecedented efficiency and secrecy. The one highlights how terrorist organizations leverage these technologies to evade detection and amplify their reach. This digital battleground necessitates a robust cyber counterterrorism strategy that includes monitoring online activities, disrupting terrorist networks, and countering extremist content with positive narratives.

The role of intelligence in preventing terrorism cannot be overstated. Effective intelligence gathering and analysis are critical for anticipating and thwarting terrorist plots. However, the one underscores the inherent difficulties in this endeavor. Terrorist organizations are adept at maintaining operational security, using encrypted communications, and employing tactics that minimize their digital footprint. The fragmented nature of modern terrorist cells, which often operate independently rather than as part of a centralized command structure, further complicates intelligence efforts. To overcome these obstacles, intelligence agencies must adopt a collaborative approach, sharing information across national and international boundaries, and employing advanced analytical techniques to identify and interpret subtle indicators of terrorist activity.

Socio-political environments also play a crucial role in either mitigating or exacerbating the threat of terrorism. The one discusses how political instability, economic disparities, and social grievances can create fertile ground for terrorist recruitment and radicalization. In regions plagued by conflict, corruption, and poor governance, terrorist organizations can exploit these vulnerabilities to establish strongholds and expand their influence. Preventing terrorism in such contexts requires a holistic approach that addresses the root causes of instability and promotes good governance, economic development, and social cohesion. International cooperation is essential in this regard, as transnational terrorism cannot be effectively combated by any single nation alone.

The challenge of preventing lone-wolf terrorism adds another layer of complexity to counterterrorism efforts. Unlike traditional terrorist cells, lone wolves operate in isolation, making them difficult to detect and disrupt. These individuals are often self-radicalized through online content and may not exhibit the same behavioral patterns as members of organized terrorist groups. The one discusses how lone wolves represent a significant and unpredictable threat due to their autonomy and the difficulty in identifying them before they act. Preventing lone-wolf terrorism requires a combination of vigilant surveillance, community-based intervention programs, and efforts to counter extremist ideologies online.

The evolving nature of terrorist tactics presents yet another challenge. Terrorist organizations are constantly innovating, adopting new methods to circumvent security measures and achieve their objectives. The one highlights how terrorists have shifted from conventional bombings and shootings to more sophisticated tactics such as cyber-attacks, biological warfare, and the use of unmanned aerial vehicles. These tactics not only pose direct threats but also create widespread fear and disruption, amplifying the psychological impact of terrorism. Counterterrorism strategies must therefore be adaptive and forward-looking, continuously evolving to anticipate and counter new threats.

Legal and ethical considerations also complicate the prevention of terrorism. The balance between security and civil liberties is a delicate one, with counterterrorism measures often infringing on individual freedoms and privacy. The one addresses the ethical dilemmas posed by surveillance, detention, and the use of force in counterterrorism operations. It argues for a rights-based approach that upholds the rule of law while effectively addressing the terrorist threat. This approach requires robust legal frameworks that provide clear guidelines for counterterrorism activities and mechanisms for oversight and accountability.

Public perception and media influence are critical factors in the fight against terrorism. The way terrorism is portrayed in the media can shape public attitudes and influence policy decisions. The one highlights how sensationalist media coverage can amplify the fear of terrorism, leading to disproportionate responses and stigmatization of certain communities. Effective counterterrorism communication strategies are necessary to manage public perception, provide accurate information, and build trust in the measures being taken to ensure security.

Preventing terrorism also involves addressing the issue of radicalization in prisons. The one discusses how prisons can serve as breeding grounds for extremist ideologies, where inmates are exposed to radical ideas and networks. Preventing radicalization in prisons requires specialized programs that focus on rehabilitation and de-radicalization, providing inmates with alternative narratives and support systems to counter extremist influences.

International cooperation is paramount in the fight against terrorism. The transnational nature of terrorist networks means that no single country can effectively combat the threat alone. The one emphasizes the importance of global partnerships in sharing intelligence, coordinating operations, and addressing the root causes of terrorism. Multilateral organizations, such as the United Nations and regional bodies, play a crucial role in facilitating this cooperation and promoting a unified approach to counterterrorism.

To wrap up, the one explores the importance of resilience in preventing terrorism. Building societal resilience involves strengthening communities' ability to withstand and recover from terrorist attacks, both physically and psychologically. This includes enhancing emergency preparedness, promoting social cohesion, and fostering a culture of vigilance and resilience. By empowering communities to take an active role in their own security, counterterrorism efforts can become more effective and sustainable. Understanding the psychological motivations of terrorists, addressing the role of technology, improving intelligence capabilities, and fostering socio-political stability are all critical components of an effective counterterrorism strategy. The future of terrorism, as envisioned in , will continue to present new and evolving threats, necessitating ongoing innovation and collaboration in counterterrorism efforts. By adopting a holistic and forward-looking approach, societies can better protect themselves against the persistent and evolving threat of terrorism.

The hope for a future without terrorism

One of the primary factors influencing the future of terrorism is the role of technology. Advances in technology have provided terrorists with new tools and methods to plan and execute attacks. The internet, for instance, has become a critical platform for radicalization, recruitment, and the dissemination of terrorist propaganda. Social media platforms and encrypted communication apps allow terrorists to reach a global audience, often evading detection by law enforcement agencies. This digital landscape has democratized the means of radicalization, enabling lone actors to become self-radicalized without direct contact with established terrorist organizations.

However, technology also presents opportunities for counter-terrorism efforts. Artificial intelligence and machine learning algorithms can analyze vast amounts of data to identify patterns and predict potential threats. Surveillance technologies, including drones and biometric systems, enhance the capability of security agencies to monitor and respond to threats. The challenge lies in balancing these technological advancements with the protection of civil liberties and privacy rights. Effective counter-terrorism strategies must navigate this delicate balance to ensure that measures taken to prevent terrorism do not infringe upon the fundamental rights of individuals.

The psychology of terrorism is another critical aspect to consider when contemplating a future without terrorism. Understanding the motivations and psychological profiles of terrorists can provide valuable insights into preventing radicalization and deradicalization. Many terrorists are driven by a complex interplay of personal, ideological, and socio-political factors. For some, the promise of belonging to a group that offers a sense of purpose and identity is a powerful motivator. Others are driven by grievances related to political, social, or economic injustices. Addressing these underlying causes of radicalization requires a holistic approach that includes social, economic, and political reforms.

Education and community engagement are essential components of a comprehensive strategy to prevent radicalization. By fostering critical thinking skills and promoting tolerance and understanding, educational programs can help to immunize young people against extremist ideologies. Community engagement initiatives can build trust between law enforcement agencies and local communities, creating an environment where individuals feel empowered to report suspicious activities. providing alternative pathways for individuals at risk of radicalization, such as vocational training and employment opportunities, can mitigate the appeal of extremist groups.

The role of international cooperation in combating terrorism cannot be overstated. Terrorism is a transnational issue that requires a coordinated global response. Sharing intelligence, best practices, and resources among countries is crucial for effectively addressing the threat. International organizations, such as the United Nations and Interpol, play a vital role in facilitating this cooperation. Additionally, addressing the root causes of terrorism, such as poverty, inequality, and political instability, requires a global commitment to sustainable development and human rights.

The future of terrorism will also be shaped by the evolving nature of conflicts and geopolitical dynamics. The rise of non-state actors, such as terrorist organizations and insurgent groups, challenges traditional notions of warfare and security. These groups often operate in failed or failing states, exploiting weak governance and lawlessness to establish safe havens. Addressing the conditions that allow these groups to thrive requires a comprehensive approach that includes diplomatic, military, and development efforts. Strengthening governance, promoting the rule of law, and fostering economic development in fragile states are essential for preventing the emergence and growth of terrorist organizations.

Climate change and environmental degradation are emerging as significant factors that could influence the future of terrorism. Environmental stressors, such as water scarcity, food insecurity, and natural disasters, can exacerbate existing social and political tensions, creating fertile ground for radicalization and extremism. Addressing these environmental challenges through sustainable development and climate resilience strategies is crucial for reducing the risk of terrorism. climate change can lead to mass migrations and displacement, which can further destabilize regions and increase the risk of conflict and terrorism.

The impact of globalization on terrorism is another important consideration. While globalization has brought about unprecedented levels of connectivity and economic integration, it has also facilitated the spread of extremist ideologies and the movement of terrorists across borders. The globalized nature of modern society means that local conflicts and grievances can quickly become internationalized, with terrorist attacks having far-reaching implications. Combating terrorism in this context requires a nuanced understanding of the interplay between local and global factors, as well as the development of strategies that address both the symptoms and root causes of terrorism.

The role of ideology in terrorism is a complex and evolving issue. While ideology plays a central role in the recruitment and radicalization of terrorists, it is often intertwined with other factors, such as personal grievances and socio-political conditions. Ideological narratives thatFrame terrorism as a legitimate response to perceived injustices can be powerful motivators for individuals seeking to join extremist groups. Countering these narratives requires a multifaceted approach that includes challenging extremist ideologies, promoting alternative narratives, and addressing the grievances that underpin them.

The future of terrorism will also be influenced by the strategies and tactics employed by terrorist organizations. As security measures become more sophisticated, terrorists are likely to adapt and innovate, developing new methods to circumvent detection and carry out attacks. The use of unconventional tactics, such as cyber-terrorism and the deployment of chemical, biological, radiological, and nuclear (CBRN) weapons, poses significant challenges for counter-terrorism efforts. Preparing for these threats requires ongoing investment in research and development, as well as the cultivation of expertise in emerging areas of security.

Public perception and media coverage of terrorism also play a crucial role in shaping the future of terrorism. The way in which terrorist attacks are reported and framed in the media can influence public opinion and policy responses. Sensationalist and fear-inducing coverage can contribute to a climate of fear and hysteria, which can be exploited by terrorist groups to further their objectives. Responsible and balanced reporting, on the other hand, can help to contextualize the threat and promote informed public discourse. Engaging with the media to promote accurate and nuanced coverage of terrorism is an important aspect of counter-terrorism efforts.

The impact of terrorism on individuals and communities is profound and long-lasting. Beyond the immediate loss of life and destruction, terrorism can have far-reaching psychological, social, and economic consequences. Addressing the needs of victims and survivors is an essential component of the healing process. Providing psychological support, legal assistance, and economic opportunities can help to mitigate the long-term impact of terrorism on individuals and communities. fostering resilience and promoting social cohesion can help to prevent the recurrence of terrorism by strengthening the fabric of society.

In contemplating a future without terrorism, it is essential to recognize the importance of hope and resilience. While the threat of terrorism is formidable, it is not insurmountable. Through a combination of strategic, technological, and socio-political measures, it is possible to reduce the risk of terrorism and create a safer and more secure world. The journey towards a future without terrorism requires a sustained commitment to addressing the root causes of radicalization, fostering international cooperation, and promoting a culture of peace and tolerance. Addressing the multifaceted nature of terrorism requires a comprehensive and integrated approach that encompasses technology, psychology, international cooperation, and community engagement. While the path to a future without terrorism is fraught with challenges, it is a goal that is both necessary and attainable. By working together, we can create a world where the threat of terrorism is minimized, and the promise of peace and security is realized for all.

Chapter 10: Terrorism and the Internet

The use of the internet for terrorist recruitment and propaganda

One of the most significant advantages the internet offers to terrorist organizations is the ability to create and disseminate sophisticated propaganda. Online platforms, such as social media, websites, and forums, allow terrorists to craft and distribute messages that are tailored to resonate with specific audiences. These messages often include a mix of ideological narratives, calls to action, and depictions of violence designed to shock and intimidate. The use of multimedia, including videos, graphics, and interactive content, enhances the appeal of these messages, making them more engaging and persuasive. By leveraging the internet's multimedia capabilities, terrorist groups can create compelling narratives that glorify their cause and attract sympathizers.

Terrorist groups also exploit the internet's anonymity and reach to radicalize individuals who might otherwise remain disconnected from extremist ideologies. Online forums and chat rooms provide spaces where individuals can engage with like-minded people, share extremist views, and be gradually indoctrinated into terrorist ideologies. This process of radicalization is often subtle and incremental, with terrorists using persuasive techniques to slowly draw individuals into their fold. The internet facilitates this by providing a constant stream of extremist content that reinforces and deepens radical beliefs. As individuals spend more time consuming this content, they become more susceptible to radicalization and more likely to support or engage in terrorist activities.

Social media platforms play a crucial role in modern terrorist recruitment strategies. These platforms are designed to connect people and facilitate the spread of information, making them ideal tools for terrorists seeking to expand their influence. Terrorists use social media to identify and engage with potential recruits, often targeting individuals who express dissatisfaction with their lives or harbor grievances against certain groups or governments. By engaging these individuals in conversation, terrorists can assess their susceptibility to radicalization and gradually introduce them to extremist ideologies. Social media algorithms, which prioritize engaging content, can inadvertently amplify terrorist messages, exposing more people to extremist ideologies and increasing the likelihood of recruitment.

The use of encrypted communication channels is another critical aspect of terrorist activities online. Platforms offering end-to-end encryption, such as Telegram and WhatsApp, allow terrorists to communicate securely, away from the prying eyes of law enforcement and intelligence agencies. These encrypted channels are used for planning attacks, disseminating instructions, and coordinating activities without the risk of interception. The anonymity provided by these platforms makes it difficult for authorities to track and disrupt terrorist networks, allowing terrorist groups to operate with relative impunity. The use of encrypted communication channels also enables terrorists to share sensitive information, such as bomb-making instructions or target selection, without fear of detection.

Terrorist organizations also use the internet to fund their operations through various means, including crowdfunding and cryptocurrency. Online platforms allow terrorists to solicit donations from sympathizers around the world, providing a steady stream of financial support. Cryptocurrencies, in particular, offer a level of anonymity that traditional financial systems do not, making it easier for terrorists to move and launder money without being detected. This financial autonomy is crucial for sustaining terrorist activities, as it allows groups to procure weapons, fund training camps, and support operatives in the field. By exploiting the internet's financial tools, terrorist organizations can maintain their operations and expand their influence without relying on traditional funding sources.

The internet also serves as a repository for terrorist knowledge and resources, providing a wealth of information that can be accessed by anyone with an internet connection. Online libraries and databases contain a vast array of materials, including training manuals, ideological texts, and practical guides for conducting terrorist activities. These resources are invaluable for aspiring terrorists, offering them the knowledge and skills needed to carry out attacks. The availability of this information democratizes terrorism, allowing individuals to self-radicalize and plan attacks without direct support from a terrorist organization. This decentralized approach to terrorism poses significant challenges for law enforcement and counterterrorism efforts, as it becomes increasingly difficult to identify and neutralize threats.

The psychological impact of online terrorist propaganda cannot be overstated. The constant exposure to violent and extremist content can desensitize individuals to violence and normalize extremist ideologies. This desensitization is a critical component of radicalization, as it lowers the psychological barriers to engaging in violent behavior. Online propaganda often portrays terrorists as heroic figures fighting against oppression, appealing to individuals' desire for meaning and purpose. This narrative can be particularly compelling for marginalized individuals seeking a sense of belonging and identity. By offering a seemingly noble cause and a community of like-minded individuals, terrorist groups can attract recruits who are willing to commit acts of violence in support of their ideology.

The internet's global reach also allows terrorist groups to target specific demographics with tailored messages. For instance, terrorists can create content that appeals to the unique cultural, social, and political contexts of different regions, making their messages more relevant and persuasive. This targeted approach increases the effectiveness of recruitment efforts, as individuals are more likely to respond to messages that resonate with their personal experiences and grievances. The ability to customize

105

propaganda for different audiences demonstrates the adaptability of terrorist organizations and their sophisticated understanding of online communication strategies.

The role of online communities in terrorist recruitment and radicalization cannot be ignored. Virtual communities, formed around shared extremist beliefs, provide social support and validation for individuals on the path to radicalization. These communities offer a sense of belonging and identity, reinforcing extremist beliefs and encouraging individuals to take action in support of the group's goals. The interactions within these online communities can be a powerful motivator, as individuals seek to gain approval and recognition from their peers. This social dynamic is a crucial element of online radicalization, as it creates a feedback loop that reinforces extremist views and behaviors.

The challenge of countering online terrorist recruitment and propaganda is immense. Law enforcement and intelligence agencies must navigate a complex digital landscape, where new platforms and technologies constantly emerge. Traditional counterterrorism strategies, which often focus on physical surveillance and disruption, are less effective in the online realm. Instead, a multifaceted approach is required, combining technological solutions, such as automated content moderation and digital forensics, with psychological and social interventions. Collaboration between governments, tech companies, and civil society is essential to develop comprehensive strategies that address the root causes of radicalization and disrupt the online networks that support terrorism.

Educational initiatives are also crucial in preventing online radicalization. By promoting media literacy and critical thinking skills, individuals can be better equipped to recognize and resist extremist propaganda. Educational programs can teach people how to evaluate online content critically, understand the techniques used by terrorists to manipulate emotions and perceptions, and develop resilience against radicalization. These initiatives must be tailored to different age groups and cultural contexts, ensuring that they are effective in diverse environments. By empowering individuals with the knowledge and skills to navigate the digital landscape safely, society can reduce the appeal of terrorist ideologies and prevent the spread of extremist views.

The use of the internet for terrorist recruitment and propaganda represents a significant evolution in the tactics and strategies of terrorist organizations. The digital age has provided terrorists with powerful tools to spread their ideologies, recruit members, and coordinate activities on a global scale. Understanding the dynamics of online radicalization and developing effective countermeasures is essential for addressing the threat posed by terrorist groups in the 21st century. As technology continues to evolve, so too must the strategies to combat online terrorism, ensuring that societies remain resilient against the ever-changing tactics of terrorist organizations.

The counterterrorism measures against online terrorism

One of the primary counterterrorism strategies discussed is the implementation of stringent content moderation policies by social media platforms. These policies are designed to detect and remove terrorist content swiftly, thereby reducing the visibility and reach of extremist messages. Advanced algorithms and artificial intelligence are increasingly being used to automate this process, identifying keywords, images, and patterns associated with terrorist propaganda. However, the effectiveness of these measures is often mitigated by the adaptive nature of terrorist groups, who continuously develop new methods to evade detection. This cat-and-mouse game underscores the need for continuous improvement and adaptation of moderation tools to stay ahead of emerging threats.

In addition to automated content moderation, collaboration between governments and tech companies plays a crucial role in counterterrorism efforts. This partnership involves sharing intelligence, expertise, and technological resources to enhance the identification and removal of terrorist content. For instance, initiatives like the Global Internet Forum to Counter Terrorism (GIFCT) facilitate cooperation among major tech companies to develop best practices and share information about terrorist activities online. Such collaborative efforts are essential for creating a unified front against online terrorism, leveraging the collective strengths of both public and private sectors.

Legal frameworks also form a critical component of counterterrorism measures. Many countries have enacted laws that specifically target online terrorist activities, imposing penalties for the dissemination of extremist content and providing legal backing for the takedown of such material. These laws often include provisions for international cooperation, recognizing that online terrorism transcends national borders. However, the balance between security and civil liberties remains a contentious issue. While stringent laws can effectively curb terrorist activities, they also raise concerns about privacy, freedom of expression, and the potential for misuse. Therefore, it is imperative that these laws are crafted and implemented with careful consideration of their broader societal impacts.

Another significant strategy is the use of cyber counterterrorism operations, which involve infiltrating and disrupting online terrorist networks. These operations can include hacking into terrorist communication channels, disrupting their online infrastructure, and conducting cyberattacks against websites and platforms used by extremists. Such measures require sophisticated technical capabilities and close coordination between intelligence agencies and cybersecurity experts. The success of these operations hinges on maintaining a high level of secrecy and technological superiority over terrorist groups, who are often adept at using encryption and other technologies to protect their online activities.

Public awareness and education campaigns are also vital in the fight against online terrorism. By informing the public about the dangers of extremist content and encouraging responsible online behavior, these campaigns aim to reduce the appeal of terrorist propaganda and prevent radicalization. Educational programs in schools and communities can equip individuals with the critical thinking skills necessary to identify and reject extremist narratives. fostering a resilient and informed public can create a broader societal resistance to terrorist ideologies, thereby diminishing the potential for radicalization.

The one also explores the role of academic research in

understanding and countering online terrorism. Scholars from various disciplines, including psychology, sociology, and computer science, contribute valuable insights into the motivations and behaviors of terrorists. This research can inform the development of more effective counterterrorism strategies by providing a deeper understanding of the psychological and social factors that drive individuals towards extremism. For example, studies on the psychological profiles of terrorists can help in designing interventions that address the root causes of radicalization, while research on online behavior can enhance the detection and prevention of terrorist activities.

Furthermore, technological innovation plays a dual role in both facilitating and combating online terrorism. On one hand, terrorists exploit new technologies to enhance their operational capabilities, using encrypted communication tools, social media platforms, and even virtual reality for propaganda and recruitment. On the other hand, advancements in technology also provide counterterrorism agencies with powerful tools for monitoring, analyzing, and disrupting terrorist activities. The development of sophisticated data analytics, machine learning algorithms, and cybersecurity measures has significantly bolstered the ability to detect and respond to online terrorist threats.

The ethical dimensions of counterterrorism measures are another critical aspect discussed in the one. The use of surveillance technologies, data mining, and other intrusive methods raises ethical concerns about the balance between security and individual rights. There is a delicate balance to be struck between effectively combating terrorism and preserving fundamental freedoms. Ethical considerations must be at the forefront of policy-making and implementation to ensure that counterterrorism measures do not infringe upon civil liberties or perpetuate discrimination and bias.

International cooperation is highlighted as an essential element in addressing the global nature of online terrorism. Terrorist networks often operate across multiple countries, exploiting jurisdictional boundaries to evade detection and prosecution. Effective counterterrorism strategies require coordinated efforts between nations, including the sharing of intelligence, harmonization of legal frameworks, and joint operations. International organizations such as the United Nations and INTERPOL play a crucial role in facilitating this cooperation, providing platforms for dialogue and collaboration among member states.

The one also addresses the challenges posed by the decentralized nature of the Internet. Unlike traditional media, the Internet allows for the rapid dissemination of information across a vast and diverse network, making it difficult to control and monitor. Terrorist groups exploit this decentralization to spread their message widely and quickly, often using multiple platforms and channels to maximize their reach. Counterterrorism measures must therefore be agile and adaptable, capable of responding to the dynamic and evolving nature of online terrorism.

the one emphasizes the importance of community engagement in counterterrorism efforts. Local communities are often the first line of defense against radicalization, as they can identify and intervene in cases of extremist influence. Building trust and cooperation between law enforcement agencies and communities is crucial for effective prevention and intervention. Community-based programs that provide support and alternatives to individuals at risk of radicalization can play a significant role in reducing the appeal of terrorist ideologies.

In brief, the one discusses the future directions of counterterrorism in the digital age. As technology continues to advance, new challenges and opportunities will emerge in the fight against online terrorism. The integration of artificial intelligence, big data, and advanced analytics will likely enhance the ability to detect and prevent terrorist activities. However, these technologies also bring ethical and practical challenges that must be carefully managed. Continuous research, innovation, and adaptation will be essential for staying ahead of the evolving threat landscape and ensuring the effectiveness of counterterrorism measures. It highlights the multifaceted nature of these efforts, encompassing content moderation, legal frameworks, cyber operations, public awareness, academic research, technological innovation, ethical considerations, international cooperation, community engagement, and future directions. Addressing the complex and evolving challenge of online terrorism requires a holistic and multifaceted approach, leveraging the strengths of various stakeholders and continuously adapting to new developments. By understanding the strategies and psychology behind terrorism, and by employing a combination of technological, legal, and social measures, it is possible to effectively combat online terrorism and safeguard society against its threats.

The future of terrorism and the internet

One of the most significant impacts of the internet on terrorism is the acceleration of the radicalization process. Online platforms provide a space where individuals can be exposed to extremist ideologies with ease, often in echo chambers that reinforce and amplify radical views. Social media algorithms, designed to maximize engagement, can inadvertently push users towards extremist content by recommending increasingly radical material. This digital radicalization is often rapid and can occur without the physical presence of a recruiter, making it difficult to detect and intervene. The virtual nature of these interactions allows for the global reach of extremist ideologies, transcending geographical boundaries and creating a decentralized network of radicalized individuals.

Recruitment strategies have also adapted to the digital age, with terrorist organizations leveraging the internet to attract and indoctrinate new members. Online forums, chat rooms, and encrypted messaging apps have become critical tools for terrorist recruiters. These platforms offer a degree of anonymity that protects both recruiters and recruits from detection. The use of sophisticated multimedia content, including videos, graphics, and interactive websites, enhances the appeal of terrorist propaganda, making it more compelling and persuasive. The internet allows for the continuous and widespread dissemination of this content, ensuring that it reaches a vast audience.

The role of propaganda in terrorist strategies cannot be overstated. The internet has enabled terrorist groups to produce and distribute high-quality propaganda with relative ease. This content is designed to inspire fear, recruit new members, and justify acts of violence. The production value of terrorist propaganda has increased significantly, with professionally produced videos and well-crafted narratives that appeal to a broad audience. The internet ensures that this propaganda is accessible to anyone with an internet connection, vastly expanding its reach and impact. The ability to share and amplify this content through social media platforms further enhances its effectiveness.

Cyberterrorism represents another dimension of the future of terrorism and the internet. While traditional acts of terrorism involve physical violence, cyberterrorism involves attacks on digital infrastructure with the intent to cause disruption, damage, or fear. Cyberterrorism can target critical infrastructure, financial systems, and government networks, potentially causing widespread chaos and economic damage. The threat of cyberterrorism is particularly concerning given the increasing reliance on digital systems in modern society. As technology continues to advance, the capabilities of cyberterrorists are likely to grow, necessitating robust cybersecurity measures and international cooperation to mitigate these risks.

The use of the dark web by terrorist groups presents additional challenges for counterterrorism efforts. The dark web provides a secure and anonymous environment where terrorists can communicate, plan operations, and acquire resources without detection. This hidden part of the internet is inaccessible through conventional search engines and requires specialized software to access. The anonymity offered by the dark web makes it an ideal platform for illegal activities, including the sale of weapons, drugs, and counterfeit documents. For terrorist groups, the dark web offers a sanctuary where they can operate with impunity, making it a significant concern for law enforcement agencies.

Encrypted communication platforms pose another challenge in the fight against terrorism. While encryption is essential for protecting privacy and securing communications, it also provides terrorists with a secure means of communication. Encrypted messaging apps and email services prevent law enforcement agencies from intercepting and monitoring communications, hindering their ability to detect and prevent terrorist activities. The debate over encryption is complex, balancing the need for privacy and security against the requirements of national security and law enforcement.

As encryption technology continues to evolve, this debate is likely to intensify, with significant implications for the future of counterterrorism.

The internet also facilitates the financing of terrorist activities through various means, including crowdfunding, online fraud, and the sale of illegal goods and services. Terrorist organizations exploit the anonymity and global reach of the internet to raise funds and support their operations. Crowdfunding platforms and social media campaigns can be used to solicit donations from sympathizers worldwide. Online fraud schemes, such as phishing and identity theft, provide additional revenue streams for terrorist groups. The sale of illegal goods and services on the dark web further supplements their finances. Counterterrorism efforts must address these financial networks to disrupt the flow of funds to terrorist organizations.

The future of terrorism and the internet also involves the exploitation of emerging technologies. Artificial intelligence, machine learning, and blockchain technology present both opportunities and challenges in the context of terrorism. AI can be used to enhance the effectiveness of terrorist propaganda, automate cyberattacks, and develop sophisticated methods of evading detection. Machine learning algorithms can analyze vast amounts of data to identify potential targets and optimize attack strategies. Blockchain technology can be used to create decentralized and untraceable financial systems, complicating efforts to track and disrupt terrorist financing. As these technologies continue to develop, their potential misuse by terrorist groups must be carefully monitored and addressed.

The globalization of the internet has also facilitated the internationalization of terrorist networks. Virtual communities of like-minded individuals can form across borders, sharing information, resources, and support. This globalization of terrorism presents unique challenges for national security and international cooperation. Traditional approaches to counterterrorism, which often focus on geographical boundaries and state-centric strategies, may be inadequate in addressing the transnational nature of internet-facilitated terrorism. Effective counterterrorism efforts require a global perspective and collaborative approaches that involve sharing intelligence, coordinating responses, and developing international legal frameworks.

The psychological impact of internet-facilitated terrorism is another critical aspect to consider. The constant exposure to online extremist content can have profound effects on individuals, influencing their perceptions, attitudes, and behaviors. The anonymity of the internet can embolden individuals to express and act on radical views that they might otherwise suppress in face-to-face interactions. The echo chamber effect, where individuals are only exposed to information that reinforces their existing beliefs, can deepen radicalization and increase the likelihood of violent actions. Understanding the psychological mechanisms behind online radicalization is essential for developing effective counter-radicalization strategies.

The role of online communities in providing social support and validation for extremist views cannot be overlooked. These communities offer a sense of belonging and identity to individuals who may feel marginalized or alienated in their offline lives. The shared beliefs and experiences within these online groups reinforce extremist ideologies and can motivate individuals to engage in violent actions. The sense of camaraderie and mutual support within these communities can be a powerful motivator, making it difficult to counteract through traditional counterterrorism measures. Addressing the social and psychological needs of individuals vulnerable to radicalization is crucial for preventing the spread of extremist ideologies.

The future of terrorism and the internet also raises ethical and legal challenges. The balance between security and civil liberties is a central concern in the digital age. Counterterrorism measures that involve surveillance, data collection, and monitoring of online activities must be carefully balanced against the rights to privacy and freedom of expression. The use of predictive analytics and AI in identifying potential terrorists raises concerns about bias, accuracy, and the potential for false positives. Ensuring that counterterrorism efforts are conducted within a legal and ethical framework is essential for maintaining public trust and upholding democratic values. The internet has transformed the landscape of terrorism, providing new avenues for radicalization, recruitment, propaganda, and financing. The anonymity, reach, and speed of digital communications have enabled terrorist groups to operate with greater agility and impact. Addressing these challenges requires a multifaceted approach that combines technological innovation, international cooperation, psychological insight, and ethical considerations. As technology continues to evolve, staying ahead of the curve in understanding and countering the nexus between terrorism and the internet will be crucial for ensuring global security and stability.

Chapter 11: Terrorism and the Nuclear Threat

The potential for terrorist groups to acquire nuclear weapons

Terrorist organizations are driven by a variety of ideological, political, and strategic motivations. For some groups, the acquisition of nuclear weapons may be seen as a means to achieve their ultimate objectives, whether it be the establishment of a caliphate, the overthrow of a regime, or the imposition of their ideological vision on a broader scale. The symbolic power of nuclear weapons cannot be overstated; their possession alone can significantly elevate a group's status and instill fear far beyond conventional means. This allure is particularly potent for groups that operate under the banner of religious extremism, where apocalyptic narratives and the desire to inflict maximum damage on perceived enemies can drive their pursuit of nuclear capabilities.

The capabilities of terrorist groups vary widely, but the general consensus among experts is that most lack the technological and scientific expertise to independently develop nuclear weapons. The process of creating a nuclear device involves complex scientific knowledge, advanced engineering, and access to fissile material, all of which are typically beyond the reach of non-state actors. However, the landscape is not static. Advances in technology, the proliferation of knowledge through the internet, and the potential for state sponsorship or the exploitation of weak states with existing nuclear infrastructure can alter this calculus.

Furthermore, the possibility of recruiting or co-opting experts cannot be discounted, particularly in regions where state control is weak and corruption is rampant.

One of the most concerning pathways for terrorist groups to acquire nuclear weapons is through state sponsorship or the exploitation of state weaknesses. States with nuclear capabilities or access to nuclear materials that are experiencing internal instability, weak governance, or are sympathetic to terrorist causes pose a significant risk. In such scenarios, terrorist groups can potentially gain access to nuclear materials, expertise, or even complete weapons. The collapse of the Soviet Union, for example, raised fears about the security of its nuclear arsenal and materials, highlighting how state instability can create opportunities for non-state actors. Similarly, regions like North Korea, where the state's nuclear ambitions and internal instability intersect, present a worrisome nexus of proliferation and terrorism.

Another critical pathway is the illicit trade in nuclear materials. The black market for nuclear and radioactive materials is a persistent threat, fueled by the demand from various actors, including terrorist groups. This trade is facilitated by global networks of smugglers, corrupt officials, and weak regulatory frameworks in certain countries. The International Atomic Energy Agency (IAEA) has documented numerous incidents of attempted smuggling of nuclear materials, underscoring the ongoing threat. While most of these incidents involve small quantities or low-grade materials, the fear is that a determined and well-funded terrorist group could eventually succeed in acquiring sufficient material to construct a crude nuclear device.

The potential for insider threats within legitimate nuclear facilities is another avenue through which terrorist groups might seek to acquire nuclear capabilities. Insiders with access to sensitive information, materials, or facilities can be exploited or coerced by terrorist groups. The risk is heightened in facilities where security protocols are lax or where personnel are vulnerable to ideological radicalization or financial inducements. This insider threat is particularly challenging to mitigate, as it involves balancing the need for stringent security with the rights

117

and privacy of employees. Enhanced vetting procedures, continuous monitoring, and psychological assessments are some of the measures that can help address this risk, but they are not foolproof.

The role of cyber threats in the context of nuclear terrorism also warrants attention. Cyber attacks on nuclear facilities can disrupt operations, compromise security systems, and potentially enable the theft of nuclear materials. The increasing digitization of nuclear infrastructure, while enhancing operational efficiency, also introduces vulnerabilities that can be exploited by cyber-savvy terrorist groups or state actors supporting them. The Stuxnet worm, which targeted Iran's nuclear facilities, demonstrated the potential for cyber warfare to physically damage nuclear infrastructure. While such sophisticated attacks require significant resources and expertise, the risk of cyber-terrorism targeting nuclear facilities is a growing concern.

The international community has made significant efforts to address the threat of nuclear terrorism through various treaties, agreements, and collaborative initiatives. The Nuclear Non-Proliferation Treaty (NPT), the Convention on the Physical Protection of Nuclear Material (CPPNM), and the Global Initiative to Combat Nuclear Terrorism (GICNT) are among the key frameworks aimed at preventing nuclear terrorism. These efforts focus on securing nuclear materials, enhancing international cooperation, and strengthening the legal and regulatory frameworks governing nuclear activities. However, the effectiveness of these measures is contingent on universal adherence and robust implementation, which remains a challenge in a world marked by diverse political interests and varying levels of state capacity.

The human element is also a critical factor in assessing the threat of nuclear terrorism. The psychology of terrorist groups, their decision-making processes, and the radicalization pathways of individuals within these groups are essential to understanding and countering the threat. Terrorist groups are not monolithic entities; they comprise individuals with varying levels of commitment, expertise, and willingness to engage in extreme violence. The radicalization process, often driven by a combination of personal grievances, ideological indoctrination, and social dynamics, plays a crucial role in determining the trajectory of a group's activities. Addressing the root causes of radicalization, enhancing community resilience, and countering extremist narratives are vital components of a comprehensive strategy to prevent nuclear terrorism.

The threat of nuclear terrorism also intersects with broader geopolitical dynamics. The relationships between states, particularly those involving nuclear powers and their allies, play a significant role in shaping the threat landscape. Alliances, rivalries, and regional conflicts can create environments conducive to nuclear proliferation and terrorism. For instance, the geopolitical tensions in regions like the Middle East, South Asia, and the Korean Peninsula are characterized by complex interactions between state and non-state actors, where the risk of nuclear materials falling into the wrong hands is heightened. Understanding these geopolitical dynamics is crucial for developing effective strategies to mitigate the threat of nuclear terrorism. The motivations, capabilities, and pathways through which terrorist groups might seek to acquire nuclear weapons are varied and complex. Addressing this threat involves not only securing nuclear materials and enhancing international cooperation but also understanding the psychological and ideological drivers of terrorism, the role of state sponsorship, the risks posed by cyber threats, and the broader geopolitical context. A concerted global effort, combining stringent security measures, effective international cooperation, and targeted efforts to counter radicalization and extremism, is essential to mitigate the risk of nuclear terrorism and safeguard global security.

The consequences of a nuclear terrorist attack

Beyond the immediate physical and psychological impacts, the environmental consequences would be severe. Radioactive fallout would contaminate large areas, rendering them uninhabitable for years or even decades. The spread of radioactive particles through air and water would lead to long-term health risks, including increased rates of cancer and genetic mutations. Agriculture and water supplies would be severely affected, potentially leading to food shortages and further health complications. The economic impact of such contamination would be devastating, with significant costs associated with decontamination efforts, healthcare, and loss of productivity.

The political and social ramifications of a nuclear terrorist attack would be equally profound. The attack would likely lead to a significant erosion of public trust in government and law enforcement agencies. The perceived inability to prevent such a catastrophic event could result in widespread social unrest and civil disobedience. Governments might respond with stringent security measures, potentially leading to a loss of civil liberties and increased surveillance. This could further strain the relationship between the state and its citizens, fostering a climate of fear and mistrust.

Internationally, the attack could lead to significant geopolitical instability. The country targeted by the attack might respond with aggressive military actions against the perceived state sponsors of terrorism. This could escalate into broader conflicts, potentially involving nuclear-armed states. The risk of nuclear retaliation and the possibility of a broader nuclear conflict would pose an existential threat to global security. The international community would likely see increased tensions and a breakdown of diplomatic relations, complicating efforts to address other global challenges such as climate change and pandemics.

The economic consequences of a nuclear terrorist attack would be profound and far-reaching. The immediate destruction of infrastructure and loss of life would disrupt economic activities, leading to a significant decline in productivity. The long-term costs of decontamination, healthcare, and rebuilding would place an enormous strain on national and global economies. Financial markets would likely experience severe volatility, with investors losing confidence in the affected country's ability to recover. The overall economic impact could lead to a global recession or depression, exacerbating existing economic inequalities and leading to widespread poverty and unemployment.

The attack would also have significant implications for global trade and supply chains. The contamination of key transportation routes and ports would disrupt the flow of goods, leading to shortages and price increases. The global economy, already interconnected and interdependent, would struggle to adapt to such a massive disruption. The resulting economic instability could lead to protectionist policies and a decline in international trade, further exacerbating the economic downturn. The long-term economic consequences would be felt globally, affecting both developed and developing countries.

The psychological impact on global populations would be another significant consequence. The fear of further attacks would lead to heightened anxiety and a pervasive sense of insecurity. This could result in changes in behavior, with individuals and communities becoming more insular and distrustful of outsiders. The media's role in shaping public perception would be crucial, with the potential for sensationalism and misinformation to exacerbate fear and panic. The long-term psychological effects would likely manifest in increased rates of mental health issues, substance abuse, and social isolation.

The attack would also challenge the ethical and moral frameworks of societies. The use of nuclear weapons, even by non-state actors, would raise profound ethical questions about the use of force and the value of human life. The indiscriminate nature of nuclear weapons, which do not distinguish between combatants and civilians, would lead to widespread condemnation and calls for accountability. The international community would likely push for stricter controls on nuclear materials and stronger measures to prevent their proliferation. The moral and ethical implications of the attack would reverberate through legal, political, and social systems, prompting debates about the balance between security and civil liberties.

In terms of national security, the attack would necessitate a reevaluation of existing counterterrorism strategies. Governments would likely invest heavily in intelligence gathering, surveillance, and law enforcement capabilities. The focus would shift towards preventing the acquisition and smuggling of nuclear materials by terrorist groups. This could lead to increased cooperation between countries in sharing intelligence and coordinating efforts to disrupt terrorist networks. However, the challenge of balancing security measures with the protection of civil liberties would remain a contentious issue, requiring careful consideration and public debate.

The attack would also have profound implications for international law and global governance. The existing legal frameworks governing nuclear non-proliferation and counterterrorism would likely be scrutinized and potentially reformed. The international community would seek to strengthen mechanisms for preventing the spread of nuclear materials and enhancing cooperation in addressing terrorism. This could involve the creation of new international treaties and the establishment of specialized agencies tasked with monitoring and enforcing compliance. The challenge would be to balance the need for robust security measures with the protection of individual rights and freedoms.

The response to a nuclear terrorist attack would also involve significant humanitarian efforts. The immediate priority would be to provide medical care and support to survivors, including psychological counseling and long-term rehabilitation. The scale of the disaster would require a coordinated international response, with aid agencies, non-governmental organizations, and foreign governments playing a crucial role. The humanitarian effort would need to address the long-term needs of affected communities, including rebuilding infrastructure, restoring livelihoods, and promoting social cohesion. The challenge would be to ensure that the response is effective, equitable, and sensitive to the needs of diverse populations.

The attack would also necessitate a rethinking of energy policies and the role of nuclear power. The risk of nuclear materials falling into the hands of terrorists would prompt a reassessment of the security measures in place at nuclear facilities. Governments might consider phasing out nuclear power in favor of alternative energy sources, or implementing stricter regulations to enhance security and prevent theft or sabotage. The debate over nuclear energy would involve balancing the benefits of clean energy with the risks of nuclear proliferation and terrorism. The outcome of this debate would have significant implications for global energy policies and the fight against climate change.

The attack would also impact international relations and diplomacy.

The targeted country would likely seek to hold the perpetrators and their sponsors accountable, leading to potential diplomatic conflicts and sanctions. The international community would need to navigate complex geopolitical dynamics to address the root causes of terrorism and prevent future attacks. This would involve addressing issues such as political instability, economic inequality, and social injustice, which can contribute to the rise of extremist ideologies. The challenge would be to build a global consensus on the need for comprehensive and coordinated efforts to counter terrorism and promote peace and stability. The immediate physical and psychological impacts would be followed by long-term environmental, economic, and social challenges. The attack would pose significant threats to global security, stability, and governance, requiring a coordinated and comprehensive international response. The ethical, moral, and legal implications would prompt profound debates about the balance between security and civil liberties. The humanitarian efforts needed to address the aftermath of the attack would require sustained commitment and cooperation from the international community. Ultimately, the prevention of such an attack would depend on the ability of governments and international organizations to address the root causes of terrorism and enhance global security measures.

The counterterrorism measures against nuclear terrorism

One of the primary counterterrorism strategies discussed is the enhancement of physical security at nuclear facilities. This includes the deployment of advanced surveillance systems, biometric access controls, and the use of robust physical barriers. These measures are designed to deter and detect any unauthorized access to nuclear materials. The integration of these security systems is complemented by rigorous training programs for personnel to ensure that they can effectively respond to potential security breaches. By strengthening the physical security of nuclear facilities, governments aim to create a formidable barrier against terrorist attempts to acquire nuclear materials.

Another critical measure involves the strengthening of international cooperation and information sharing. Nuclear terrorism is a transnational threat that requires a coordinated global response. Countries must work together to share intelligence, track the movement of nuclear materials, and collaborate on joint operations to intercept illicit nuclear trafficking. The establishment of international frameworks, such as the Nuclear Security Summit process, facilitates this cooperation by bringing together world leaders to commit to specific actions aimed at enhancing nuclear security. These summits have resulted in tangible outcomes, such as the removal of highly enriched uranium from several countries and the improvement of global nuclear security standards.

The implementation of stringent regulations and oversight mechanisms for the handling and transportation of nuclear materials is also a key counterterrorism strategy. Governments must ensure that all nuclear materials are accounted for and securely transported. This involves the creation of comprehensive inventory systems and the use of secure transportation methods. Additionally, regulatory bodies must conduct regular inspections and audits to ensure compliance with security protocols. By enforcing strict regulations, authorities can minimize the risk of nuclear materials falling into the wrong hands due to negligence or corruption.

The development and deployment of advanced technologies play a crucial role in counterterrorism efforts against nuclear terrorism. Technologies such as radiation detection devices and nuclear forensics capabilities are essential for identifying and tracking nuclear materials. Radiation detection portals at border crossings and major transit hubs enable authorities to detect the presence of radioactive materials in cargo and luggage. Nuclear forensics, on the other hand, allows investigators to trace the origin of intercepted nuclear materials, providing valuable intelligence on the source and potential routes of nuclear smuggling networks.

In addition to technological advancements, counterterrorism strategies must also address the human element of nuclear security. This involves the implementation of rigorous vetting processes for personnel working in the nuclear industry. Background checks, security clearances, and continuous monitoring are essential to prevent individuals with malicious intent from infiltrating nuclear facilities. Furthermore, ongoing training and education programs are necessary to ensure that personnel are aware of the latest security protocols and are prepared to respond to potential threats.

The role of intelligence and counterintelligence operations cannot be overstated in the fight against nuclear terrorism. Intelligence agencies must actively gather information on terrorist groups' intentions and capabilities regarding nuclear materials. This includes monitoring communications, infiltrating terrorist networks, and conducting covert operations to gather actionable intelligence. Counterintelligence efforts are equally important, as they aim to identify and neutralize threats from within, such as insider threats or espionage activities that could compromise nuclear security.

Public awareness and engagement are also vital components of counterterrorism strategies. Educating the public about the risks of nuclear terrorism and the importance of nuclear security can foster a culture of vigilance. Community-based programs can empower citizens to report suspicious activities and contribute to broader security efforts. transparent communication from authorities regarding nuclear security measures can build public trust and cooperation, which are essential for the success of counterterrorism initiatives.

The deterrence of nuclear terrorism also involves the use of legal and policy frameworks to criminalize activities related to the illicit acquisition and use of nuclear materials. International treaties, such as the Treaty on the Non-Proliferation of Nuclear Weapons (NPT) and the Convention on the Physical Protection of Nuclear Material (CPPNM), establish legal obligations for states to protect nuclear materials and prevent their illicit transfer. These treaties also provide mechanisms for international cooperation in the investigation and prosecution of nuclear terrorism cases. By strengthening the legal framework, countries can create a deterrent effect that makes it more difficult for terrorist groups to operate with impunity.

Counterterrorism measures must also consider the potential for cyber threats to nuclear security. The increasing reliance on digital systems for the operation and management of nuclear facilities presents new vulnerabilities that could be exploited by cyber terrorists. Ensuring the cybersecurity of nuclear facilities involves the implementation of robust cyber defense mechanisms, such as firewalls, intrusion detection systems, and encryption protocols. Regular cybersecurity assessments and the development of incident response plans are essential to protect nuclear facilities from cyber-attacks that could compromise their security.

The psychological aspect of counterterrorism is another important dimension. Understanding the motivations and psychological profiles of individuals involved in nuclear terrorism can inform the development of effective counter-radicalization and de-radicalization programs. Psychological profiling can help identify individuals who may be susceptible to radicalization and recruitment by terrorist groups. Interventions aimed at addressing the underlying psychological and social factors that contribute to radicalization can prevent individuals from pursuing nuclear terrorism.

In addition to preventive measures, preparedness and response capabilities are crucial components of counterterrorism strategies. Governments must develop comprehensive emergency response plans to address potential nuclear terrorism incidents. These plans should include protocols for evacuation, medical response, and decontamination in the event of a nuclear attack or accident. Regular drills and exercises are necessary to ensure that response teams are well-prepared to handle such incidents. Effective communication and coordination between different agencies and levels of government are also essential for a successful response.

The financial aspect of counterterrorism efforts cannot be overlooked. Adequate funding is necessary to support the implementation of comprehensive security measures, research and development of new technologies, and international cooperation initiatives. Governments must allocate sufficient resources to nuclear security programs and ensure that these resources are used effectively. Private sector engagement is also important, as many nuclear facilities are operated by private companies. Public-private partnerships can leverage the expertise and resources of the private sector to enhance nuclear security.

The ethical considerations of counterterrorism measures must be carefully balanced with security imperatives. While robust security measures are necessary, they must not infringe on civil liberties and human rights. The use of surveillance technologies, for example, must be conducted in a manner that respects privacy and is subject to appropriate oversight. Transparency and accountability in the implementation of counterterrorism measures are essential to maintain public trust and ensure that security efforts are perceived as legitimate and fair. From enhancing physical security and international cooperation to leveraging advanced technologies and addressing the human element, these measures are designed to create a comprehensive and resilient defense against the nuclear threat. The effectiveness of these measures depends on the continuous adaptation and improvement of strategies in response to evolving threats and the commitment of governments, international organizations, and civil society to prioritize nuclear security. By addressing the multifaceted nature of nuclear terrorism, counterterrorism efforts can mitigate the risks and protect global security.

Chapter 12: Terrorism and the Biological Threat

The potential for terrorist groups to acquire biological weapons

One of the primary factors contributing to the potential acquisition of biological weapons by terrorist groups is the widespread availability of dual-use technologies. Many biotechnological tools and equipment, which are essential for legitimate scientific research and medical advancements, can also be repurposed for malicious purposes. For instance, the same equipment used to produce vaccines and therapeutic proteins can be used to cultivate and disseminate biological agents. This duality presents a formidable challenge for regulators and law enforcement agencies, as restricting access to these technologies can impede scientific progress and medical research. Consequently, the accessibility of such technologies necessitates a delicate balance between fostering innovation and implementing stringent safeguards to prevent misuse.

the global nature of scientific research and the ease of international travel further complicate efforts to prevent the proliferation of biological weapons. The collaborative nature of modern science means that knowledge and expertise are frequently shared across borders, increasing the risk that sensitive information could fall into the wrong hands. Terrorist groups may exploit this interconnectedness by recruiting individuals with specialized knowledge or by infiltrating legitimate research institutions. The possibility of insider threats within scientific and medical communities underscores the need for robust security measures and comprehensive background checks to mitigate the risk of biological weapon proliferation.

The appeal of biological weapons to terrorist groups also stems from their potential to cause disproportionate levels of fear and disruption relative to their actual use. Unlike conventional weapons, the psychological impact of a biological attack can far exceed the immediate physical damage. The invisible and often delayed nature of biological agents can create widespread panic and mistrust, leading to significant social and economic consequences. The 2001 anthrax attacks in the United States, for example, caused widespread fear and disruption despite resulting in a relatively small number of casualties. This disproportionate impact can be a powerful motivator for terrorist groups seeking to maximize their influence and achieve their objectives.

Additionally, the perceived simplicity and cost-effectiveness of biological weapons compared to other forms of weaponry make them an attractive option for terrorist organizations. Developing and deploying biological agents can be significantly less expensive than acquiring or producing conventional explosives or nuclear devices. The relative ease of production, combined with the potential for mass casualties, makes biological weapons a cost-effective means of achieving large-scale impact. This economic efficiency is particularly appealing to non-state actors with limited resources, enabling them to pursue high-impact attacks without the need for extensive logistical support or financial backing.

The threat is further amplified by the potential for state sponsorship of terrorist groups seeking to acquire biological weapons. Some rogue states may view supporting terrorist organizations as a means to advance their own strategic objectives without directly implicating themselves in acts of terrorism. The transfer of biological agents or technical expertise from state actors to terrorist groups can significantly enhance the capabilities of these non-state actors, enabling them to carry out sophisticated attacks with potentially devastating consequences. The nexus between state actors and terrorist groups underscores the importance of international cooperation and intelligence sharing to identify and disrupt such collaborations.

The potential for terrorist groups to acquire biological weapons is also heightened by the increasing accessibility of information on the internet. Detailed instructions on how to produce and deploy biological agents are readily available online, providing aspiring terrorists with the knowledge necessary to carry out attacks. The proliferation of online forums and dark web marketplaces facilitates the exchange of information and materials among like-minded individuals, creating a virtual breeding ground for terrorist activities. Efforts to counter this threat must include robust cyber security measures and international collaboration to monitor and regulate online activities that could contribute to the proliferation of biological weapons.

Furthermore, the evolving nature of biological threats requires continuous adaptation and innovation in security strategies. Traditional approaches to counter-terrorism, which often focus on preventing attacks using explosives or firearms, may be insufficient to address the complexities of biological threats. The development of early warning systems, rapid response capabilities, and effective medical countermeasures is essential to mitigate the impact of a biological attack. Investing in research and development of new technologies for detection, prevention, and treatment of biological agents is critical to staying ahead of the evolving threat landscape.

The potential for terrorist groups to acquire biological weapons also highlights the importance of international cooperation and information sharing. The global nature of the threat necessitates a coordinated response that transcends national borders. International treaties and agreements, such as the Biological Weapons Convention, provide a framework for cooperation and accountability among nations. Strengthening these agreements and ensuring compliance through rigorous verification mechanisms are essential to prevent the proliferation of biological weapons. Additionally, fostering collaboration between intelligence agencies, law enforcement, and public health organizations can enhance the ability to detect and respond to biological threats in a timely and effective manner.

The role of public health systems in countering the threat of biological weapons cannot be overstated. Robust public health infrastructure is critical for early detection and response to biological attacks. Enhanced surveillance systems, rapid diagnostic capabilities, and effective communication channels are essential components of a comprehensive public health strategy. Additionally, training healthcare professionals to recognize and respond to unusual disease patterns can improve the timely identification of a biological attack. Integrating public health and security efforts ensures a coordinated and efficient response to potential biological threats, minimizing their impact on society. The accessibility of dual-use technologies, the global nature of scientific research, the disproportionate impact of biological attacks, the economic efficiency of biological weapons, and the potential for state sponsorship all contribute to the complexity of this threat. Addressing these challenges necessitates a combination of technological innovation, international cooperation, robust public health infrastructure, and effective security measures. By adopting a holistic and collaborative approach, the international community can enhance its ability to prevent and respond to the threat of biological terrorism, safeguarding global security and public health.

The consequences of a biological terrorist attack

One of the most immediate and palpable consequences of a biological terrorist attack is the direct impact on public health. Biological agents such as anthrax, smallpox, or a highly contagious virus like influenza can cause significant morbidity and mortality. The lethality of these agents varies, but even those with lower fatality rates can overwhelm healthcare systems due to the sheer number of affected individuals requiring care. For instance, an attack involving a weaponized strain of smallpox could rapidly exhaust medical resources, given that smallpox has a high transmission rate and a significant portion of the population lacks immunity. This scenario necessitates a surge in healthcare services, including hospital beds, medical personnel, and pharmaceuticals, which may not be readily available.

Beyond the immediate health impacts, biological attacks can induce long-term health consequences. Survivors may suffer from chronic conditions or disabilities, necessitating ongoing medical care and support. The psychological trauma experienced by those directly affected, as well as the broader community, can lead to long-term mental health issues, such as anxiety, depression, and post-traumatic stress disorder (PTSD). The widespread fear of contagion can lead to behavioral changes, such as avoidance of public spaces and social interactions, which can have profound effects on community cohesion and mental health.

The economic consequences of a biological terrorist attack are substantial and multifaceted. Direct costs include the immediate expenses related to emergency response, medical treatment, and decontamination efforts. Indirect costs arise from disruptions to economic activities, such as business closures, supply chain interruptions, and reduced consumer confidence. The tourism and travel industries are particularly vulnerable, as fear of contagion can lead to a sharp decline in international and domestic travel. For example, an attack in a major urban center could lead to the imposition of quarantines and travel restrictions, severely impacting local and global economies.

the financial markets are highly sensitive to the uncertainty and fear generated by biological terrorist attacks. A significant attack could trigger a stock market crash, as investors react to the potential for prolonged economic disruption. The costs associated with increased security measures, research and development of vaccines and treatments, and compensation for affected individuals and businesses further strain public and private finances. These economic impacts can lead to job losses, reduced income, and increased poverty, exacerbating social inequalities and contributing to social instability.

The social consequences of a biological terrorist attack are profound and far-reaching. Trust in public institutions and government can erode rapidly if the response is perceived as inadequate or incompetent. Misinformation and conspiracy theories can proliferate, further undermining public trust and complicating efforts to manage the crisis effectively. The stigmatization of

132

certain groups, based on ethnicity, nationality, or religion, can lead to social divisions and conflict. This was evident during the COVID-19 pandemic, where xenophobia and discrimination against Asian communities increased globally.

The erosion of social trust can also affect community resilience and the ability to mount a coordinated response to future threats. In a highly interconnected world, the impact of a biological terrorist attack can extend beyond national borders, affecting international relations and cooperation. Countries may impose strict border controls and travel restrictions, leading to a decline in global trade and cooperation. The resulting isolation can hinder the global response to the attack, delaying the development and distribution of vaccines and treatments.

The psychological impact of a biological terrorist attack cannot be overstated. The fear of invisible and potentially deadly agents creates a pervasive sense of vulnerability and helplessness. This fear can lead to widespread panic and irrational behavior, such as hoarding of supplies, which exacerbates shortages and contributes to social unrest. The constant threat of contagion can lead to chronic stress and anxiety, affecting mental health and overall well-being.

Furthermore, the psychological impact is not limited to those directly affected by the attack. Media coverage and public discourse about the attack can amplify fear and anxiety, even in individuals who are not at immediate risk. The 24. 7 news cycle and social media can spread misinformation and sensationalize the threat, heightening public anxiety. This psychological strain can manifest in various ways, including increased rates of mental health disorders, substance abuse, and social withdrawal.

The response to a biological terrorist attack requires a coordinated and comprehensive approach involving multiple sectors and levels of government. Effective communication is crucial to maintain public trust and ensure compliance with public health measures. Transparent and timely dissemination of information about the nature of the threat, the measures being taken, and the resources available can help mitigate panic and misinformation. Engaging with community leaders and stakeholders can also enhance the effectiveness of the response by building trust and promoting cooperation.

International cooperation is essential in addressing the global nature of biological threats. Sharing information, resources, and expertise can improve the global capacity to prevent, detect, and respond to biological attacks. Strengthening international frameworks for pandemic preparedness and response, such as the International Health Regulations (IHR), can enhance global resilience to biological terrorism. Collaboration in research and development of vaccines and treatments can accelerate the availability of countermeasures, reducing the impact of an attack.

Preparedness and prevention are key components of mitigating the consequences of a biological terrorist attack. Investing in public health infrastructure, including surveillance systems, laboratory capacity, and healthcare facilities, can enhance early detection and response capabilities. Developing and stockpiling vaccines and treatments for potential biological agents can reduce the time needed to deploy effective countermeasures. Conducting regular drills and exercises can improve the readiness of healthcare systems and emergency responders to manage a biological crisis.

In addition to these measures, fostering a culture of preparedness within communities can enhance resilience. Educating the public about biological threats and promoting behaviors that reduce the risk of transmission, such as hand hygiene and vaccination, can mitigate the impact of an attack. Building strong social networks and community organizations can provide support and resources during a crisis, strengthening community resilience. Addressing these consequences requires a comprehensive and coordinated approach that integrates public health, economic, social, and psychological perspectives. Enhancing preparedness, fostering international cooperation, and building resilient communities are essential strategies for mitigating the impact of biological terrorism and ensuring a swift and effective response to such threats.

The counterterrorism measures against biological terrorism

Prevention efforts primarily focus on strengthening biosecurity and biosafety protocols to reduce the likelihood of biological agents falling into the wrong hands. This includes enhancing security measures at laboratories and research facilities where dangerous pathogens are handled. Stringent access controls, surveillance systems, and background checks for personnel are critical components of biosecurity. Additionally, regulations and guidelines are implemented to ensure safe handling, storage, and transportation of biological materials. International collaborations and agreements, such as the Biological Weapons Convention (BWC), play a crucial role in promoting global standards and cooperation to prevent the development, production, and stockpiling of biological weapons.

Surveillance and early warning systems are essential for detecting potential biological threats before they materialize into full-blown attacks. These systems involve monitoring disease outbreaks, unusual patterns of illness, and suspicious activities related to biological agents. Public health surveillance networks, veterinary surveillance, and environmental monitoring contribute to the early detection of biological threats. Advanced technologies, such as genomic sequencing and bioinformatics, enhance the capability to identify and track pathogens rapidly. Timely detection allows for swift intervention, potentially preventing a localized incident from escalating into a widespread crisis.

Intelligence gathering and analysis are pivotal in identifying and thwarting biological terrorism plots. Intelligence agencies work to gather information on potential threats, including the activities of terrorist groups, the acquisition of biological materials, and indicators of planned attacks. Human intelligence, signals intelligence, and cyber intelligence are employed to piece together a comprehensive picture of the threat landscape. Collaboration between intelligence agencies, both domestically and internationally, enhances the ability to preemptively address threats. Sharing information and coordinating efforts are crucial for staying ahead of sophisticated adversaries who may exploit global networks and resources.

In addition to prevention, preparedness involves developing robust response capabilities to manage and mitigate the consequences of a biological attack. This includes training and equipping first responders, healthcare professionals, and emergency management personnel to handle biological incidents. Preparedness efforts focus on ensuring rapid identification, containment, and treatment of affected individuals. Stockpiling of medical countermeasures, such as vaccines and antibiotics, is a critical aspect of preparedness. These stockpiles must be maintained and regularly updated to address emerging biological threats.

Public health infrastructure plays a central role in the response to biological terrorism. Strengthening public health systems ensures that they are capable of handling the surge in demand for medical care and the need for widespread distribution of countermeasures during an outbreak. This includes enhancing laboratory capacity, ensuring the availability of diagnostic tools, and maintaining surge capacity in healthcare facilities. Effective communication strategies are also essential for managing public anxiety and ensuring that accurate information is disseminated promptly.

The legal and regulatory framework supporting counterterrorism measures against biological terrorism is another critical component. National laws and regulations must provide the necessary authority for preventive and responsive actions. This includes laws related to biosecurity, public health emergency powers, and the regulation of dangerous biological materials. International legal instruments, such as the BWC and the United Nations Security Council Resolution 1540, provide a framework for global cooperation and accountability. Ensuring compliance with these agreements and strengthening their implementation are essential for a coordinated global response to biological threats.

Education and awareness programs are vital for enhancing public understanding of biological threats and promoting community resilience. These programs aim to inform the public about the nature of biological threats, the importance of preventive measures, and the appropriate responses in the event of an incident. By fostering a well-informed public, these programs contribute to a culture of vigilance and preparedness. Community engagement initiatives also play a role in building trust and cooperation between the public and authorities, which is essential for effective response efforts.

Technological advancements and innovation are continually shaping the landscape of counterterrorism measures against biological terrorism. Emerging technologies, such as synthetic biology and gene editing, present both opportunities and challenges. While these technologies hold promise for developing new medical countermeasures and enhancing biosecurity, they also pose risks if misused. Efforts to regulate and monitor the use of these technologies are necessary to prevent their potential exploitation for malicious purposes. Additionally, advancements in artificial intelligence and machine learning are being leveraged to improve threat detection, data analysis, and decision-making processes in counterterrorism efforts.

International cooperation and partnerships are fundamental to addressing the transnational nature of biological threats. Biological terrorism knows no borders, and effective counterterrorism measures require coordinated efforts across countries. Regional and global initiatives, such as the Global Health Security Agenda (GHSA), promote collaboration in building capacities to prevent, detect, and respond to biological threats. Sharing best practices, technical expertise, and resources enhances the collective ability to combat biological terrorism. Strengthening the capacity of low- and middle-income countries to manage biological risks is particularly important, as these regions may be more vulnerable to biological attacks and outbreaks.

The role of non-governmental organizations (NGOs) and the private sector is also significant in counterterrorism measures against biological terrorism. NGOs often provide critical support in areas such as public health, emergency response, and community engagement. Their expertise and local knowledge can enhance the effectiveness of counterterrorism efforts. The private sector, including biotechnology companies and pharmaceutical manufacturers, plays a crucial role in developing and producing medical countermeasures. Partnerships between the public and private sectors facilitate the rapid development and deployment of these

137

countermeasures in the event of a biological attack.

Evaluating and improving counterterrorism measures is an ongoing process. Regular assessments of the effectiveness of current strategies and the identification of gaps and vulnerabilities are essential for continuous improvement. Exercises and drills, involving multiple stakeholders, help test the readiness and coordination of response efforts. After-action reviews following real or simulated incidents provide valuable insights into the strengths and weaknesses of the response. Incorporating lessons learned into future planning and preparedness efforts ensures that counterterrorism measures remain robust and adaptive to evolving threats. Strengthening biosecurity, enhancing surveillance and early warning systems, improving intelligence gathering and analysis, and developing robust response capabilities are central to these measures. The legal and regulatory framework, education and awareness programs, technological advancements, and international cooperation all play crucial roles in enhancing the effectiveness of counterterrorism efforts. Continuous evaluation and improvement are necessary to ensure that these measures remain effective in addressing the evolving nature of biological threats. By adopting a holistic and collaborative approach, the global community can better protect itself against the devastating consequences of biological terrorism.

Chapter 13:
Terrorism and the
Chemical Threat

The potential for terrorist groups to acquire chemical weapons

Chemical weapons, by their very nature, pose a unique threat due to their ability to inflict mass casualties and induce widespread panic with relatively small quantities. Unlike conventional weapons, chemical agents can be dispersed over large areas, affecting both military and civilian populations indiscriminately. This indiscriminate nature aligns with the goals of many terrorist organizations seeking to maximize fear and disruption. The psychological impact of chemical attacks can be profound, creating a sense of vulnerability and helplessness among the populace, which can be leveraged by terrorist groups to amplify their message and achieve their objectives.

The history of chemical warfare and terrorism provides valuable insights into the motivations and capabilities of terrorist groups seeking these weapons. Notable incidents, such as the 1995 sarin gas attack on the Tokyo subway by the Aum Shinrikyo cult, illustrate the devastating potential of chemical terrorism. This attack, which resulted in numerous fatalities and thousands of injuries, underscored the lethal efficiency of chemical agents and the challenges in detecting and preventing such incidents. The Aum Shinrikyo's ability to produce sarin gas in a relatively sophisticated laboratory setting highlights the feasibility of non-state actors acquiring and utilizing chemical weapons.

The motivations behind terrorist groups seeking chemical weapons are multifaceted. For some, the primary goal is to inflict maximum casualties and create a spectacle that garners international attention. For others, the use of chemical weapons serves as a means to achieve strategic objectives, such as coercing governments or destabilizing societies. The pursuit of chemical weapons can also be driven by ideological imperatives, where the use of such weapons is seen as a justified means to an end. Understanding these motivations is crucial for developing effective counter-terrorism strategies that address the root causes and underlying drivers of chemical terrorism.

The accessibility of chemical precursors is a critical factor in the potential for terrorist groups to acquire chemical weapons. Many of the chemicals used in the production of chemical agents have legitimate industrial and commercial applications, making them widely available. This dual-use nature complicates regulatory efforts, as restricting access to these chemicals can have significant economic and societal impacts. The challenge lies in balancing the need for security with the necessity of maintaining legitimate industrial and scientific activities. Effective regulation must focus on monitoring and controlling the sale and distribution of key precursors without unduly hindering legitimate uses.

The internet plays a significant role in the dissemination of knowledge related to chemical weapons. The proliferation of online resources, including detailed instructions on the synthesis and deployment of chemical agents, lowers the barriers for extremist groups seeking to acquire these capabilities. The dark web, in particular, provides a platform for the exchange of illicit information and materials, enabling terrorist groups to operate with a degree of anonymity. Counter-terrorism efforts must therefore include robust cyber strategies to monitor and disrupt these activities, preventing the transfer of knowledge and materials that could facilitate chemical attacks.

The role of state actors in the proliferation of chemical weapons is another critical consideration. Some states may knowingly or unwittingly provide support to terrorist groups seeking chemical capabilities. This support can take various forms, including the supply of precursor chemicals, technical expertise, or safe havens for training and production. The nexus between state and non-state actors in the realm of chemical terrorism poses a complex challenge for international security. Addressing this issue requires a multifaceted approach that includes diplomatic efforts to curb state sponsorship, intelligence sharing, and international cooperation to monitor and interdict illicit transfers.

The development and deployment of chemical weapons by terrorist groups also raise significant ethical and legal questions. The use of chemical agents in warfare is prohibited under international law, specifically the Chemical Weapons Convention (CWC), which aims to eliminate the development, production, stockpiling, and use of chemical weapons. Terrorist groups, by their very nature, operate outside the bounds of international law, making their acquisition and use of chemical weapons particularly egregious. Strengthening international legal frameworks and enhancing cooperation among states are essential steps in ensuring that those who facilitate or engage in chemical terrorism are held accountable.

The potential for terrorist groups to acquire chemical weapons is not uniform across all extremist organizations. Some groups may lack the technical expertise, resources, or organizational structure necessary to develop and deploy these weapons effectively. Assessing the threat level requires a nuanced understanding of the specific capabilities and intentions of different terrorist organizations. This assessment must be dynamic, continuously updated based on intelligence and situational awareness. Effective counter-terrorism strategies must be tailored to address the varying levels of threat posed by different groups, focusing resources on those with the highest potential to acquire and use chemical weapons.

Preventing terrorist groups from acquiring chemical weapons requires a comprehensive and multi-layered approach. This includes robust intelligence gathering and analysis to identify and interdict potential threats, stringent regulation and monitoring of chemical precursors, and international cooperation to address the transnational nature of the threat. Public awareness and education are also crucial components, as informed communities are better equipped to recognize and report suspicious activities. Additionally, fostering resilience within societies to withstand and recover from potential chemical attacks is essential in mitigating the broader impact of chemical terrorism.

The role of technology in both facilitating and countering the threat of chemical terrorism cannot be overstated. Advances in detection technologies, such as sensors and monitoring systems, enhance the ability to identify and respond to chemical threats in real-time. Similarly, developments in data analytics and artificial intelligence can improve the ability to predict and prevent attacks by analyzing patterns and identifying potential threats before they materialize. Investing in research and development of these technologies is crucial in staying ahead of the evolving threat landscape.

International cooperation and information sharing are paramount in addressing the global nature of the chemical terrorism threat. Terrorist groups often operate across borders, exploiting weak points in international security regimes. Effective counter-terrorism efforts require a coordinated approach, with countries working together to share intelligence, harmonize regulations, and conduct joint operations. Multilateral organizations, such as the United Nations and the Organization for the Prohibition of Chemical Weapons (OPCW), play a vital role in facilitating this cooperation and ensuring a unified response to the threat of chemical terrorism.

The potential for terrorist groups to acquire chemical weapons represents a formidable challenge that requires a concerted and sustained effort from the international community. By understanding the motivations and capabilities of these groups, enhancing regulatory frameworks, leveraging technological advancements, and fostering international cooperation, it is possible to mitigate the threat and protect societies from the devastating consequences of chemical terrorism. The task is complex and demanding, but the stakes are too high to ignore. Continued vigilance and proactive measures are essential in safeguarding against this insidious threat.

The consequences of a chemical terrorist attack

In the short term, the healthcare infrastructure bears the brunt of the impact. Hospitals and clinics face an unprecedented demand for specialized treatments and antidotes, which may be in limited supply. The need for decontamination procedures further strains resources, as victims must be thoroughly cleansed to prevent secondary contamination and to receive appropriate medical care. This surge in demand can lead to a temporary collapse of the healthcare system, particularly in regions with already strained resources. The psychological toll on healthcare workers, who are at the frontline of such crises, is also significant, potentially leading to burnout and long-term mental health issues.

Beyond the immediate medical response, the economic fallout of a chemical terrorist attack can be devastating. The contamination of public spaces and infrastructure necessitates extensive and costly decontamination efforts, which can disrupt daily life and economic activities for extended periods. Businesses, particularly those in the affected areas, may suffer from prolonged closures, leading to significant revenue losses and potential bankruptcies. The tourism industry, a vital economic sector for many regions, is particularly vulnerable as travelers avoid areas perceived as unsafe. The overall economic impact can be profound, leading to job losses and a decline in economic growth.

The psychological impact on the general population is another critical consequence. The fear and uncertainty generated by a chemical attack can lead to widespread anxiety and stress. The constant threat of another attack can create a pervasive sense of insecurity, altering people's behavior and daily routines. This heightened state of fear can erode social cohesion and trust, as individuals become more suspicious and less willing to engage in community activities. The mental health burden is substantial, with increased rates of anxiety, depression, and post-traumatic stress disorder (PTSD) among the affected population. The need for psychological support services spikes, placing additional demands on already stretched mental health resources.

the long-term health effects on survivors can be severe and

debilitating. Exposure to certain chemicals can result in chronic respiratory conditions, neurological damage, and an increased risk of cancer. The medical community must be prepared to address these long-term health issues, which may require ongoing treatment and support. The financial burden of chronic health care can be overwhelming for individuals and families, particularly in countries without comprehensive health insurance systems. The societal cost of managing these long-term health consequences can be substantial, necessitating increased investment in healthcare infrastructure and services.

The environmental impact of a chemical terrorist attack is also a significant concern. Chemical agents released into the environment can contaminate soil, water, and air, leading to long-term ecological damage. The cleanup and remediation of contaminated sites can be complex and costly, requiring specialized techniques and equipment. The potential for secondary contamination, where chemicals spread to surrounding areas through water runoff or air dispersion, complicates these efforts. The environmental degradation can have far-reaching consequences for agriculture, wildlife, and human health, as pollutants enter the food chain and water supply.

In addition to these direct impacts, a chemical terrorist attack can have profound social and political repercussions. The erosion of public trust in government and institutions is a common consequence, as citizens question the effectiveness of security measures and response efforts. This loss of trust can lead to political instability, as people demand accountability and improvements in public safety measures. Governments may face increased pressure to implement stricter security protocols, which can infringe on civil liberties and lead to debates about the balance between security and freedom. The politicization of security measures can further polarize society, creating divisions that are difficult to reconcile.

The international dimension of a chemical terrorist attack must also be considered. Such an attack can have global ramifications, affecting international relations and cooperation. Countries may impose travel bans and trade restrictions on the affected nation, leading to economic isolation and diplomatic tensions. The need for international collaboration in responding to the attack and preventing future incidents becomes crucial. Sharing intelligence, coordinating security measures, and providing mutual assistance are essential components of an effective response. However, differing national interests and priorities can complicate these efforts, highlighting the challenges of global cooperation in counterterrorism. Addressing these multifaceted impacts requires a comprehensive and coordinated approach, involving robust healthcare responses, economic support measures, psychological support services, environmental remediation efforts, and international cooperation. The complexity and severity of these consequences underscore the critical need for effective counterterrorism strategies and preparedness to mitigate the risks and protect societies from the devastating effects of such attacks.

The counterterrorism measures against chemical terrorism

One key component of prevention is the control of precursor chemicals that can be used to manufacture chemical weapons. International regulations and treaties, such as the Chemical Weapons Convention (CWC), play a significant role in this regard. The CWC prohibits the development, production, acquisition, stockpiling, retention, transfer, or use of chemical weapons. It also mandates the destruction of existing stockpiles and imposes strict verification measures to ensure compliance. Countries that are party to the CWC are required to implement domestic legislation that aligns with the treaty's provisions, thereby creating a legal framework to control the availability of dangerous chemicals.

Beyond international treaties, national laws and regulations are crucial in mitigating the risk of chemical terrorism. Governments must establish stringent controls over the production, distribution, and sale of chemicals that could be diverted for malicious use. This includes implementing licensing requirements for businesses that handle such chemicals and conducting regular inspections to ensure compliance. Additionally, there should be mechanisms in place for tracking the movement of these chemicals to prevent them from falling into the wrong hands.

Another critical aspect of counterterrorism measures is the protection of critical infrastructure. Chemical facilities, in particular, are potential targets for terrorist attacks. Therefore, it is essential to implement stringent security measures at these sites. This includes physical security measures such as fences, surveillance cameras, and access controls, as well as cyber security measures to protect against cyber-attacks that could compromise the security of chemical plants. Furthermore, employees at these facilities should receive regular training on security protocols and how to recognize and respond to suspicious activities.

In addition to preventative measures, preparedness is a key element of counterterrorism against chemical terrorism. This involves planning and exercising responses to potential chemical attacks to ensure that all relevant agencies and personnel are ready to act swiftly and effectively in the event of an incident. Preparedness efforts include the development of emergency response plans, the establishment of communication networks, and the conduct of regular drills and exercises. These activities help to identify potential weaknesses in the response system and provide opportunities to address them before an actual attack occurs.

The role of the healthcare system in preparedness cannot be overstated. Medical professionals must be trained to recognize the symptoms of exposure to chemical agents and to provide appropriate treatment. Hospitals and other healthcare facilities need to be equipped with the necessary antidotes, decontamination facilities, and protective equipment. Furthermore, there must be protocols in place for the rapid distribution of medical supplies and the coordination of medical response efforts in the aftermath of a chemical attack.

Public awareness and education are also vital components of preparedness. The public should be informed about the potential threats of chemical terrorism and the steps they can take to protect themselves. This includes providing information on how to recognize signs of a chemical attack and what actions to take in the event of an incident. Public awareness campaigns can help to reduce panic and confusion in the event of an attack, thereby facilitating a more orderly and effective response.

Response measures are the final piece of the counterterrorism puzzle. In the immediate aftermath of a chemical attack, the primary objectives are to contain the incident, provide medical care to those affected, and prevent further casualties. This requires a coordinated response involving law enforcement, emergency services, and healthcare providers. Rapid deployment of specialized units trained to handle chemical incidents is essential to mitigate the impact of the attack.

Decontamination is a critical aspect of the response effort. This involves the removal of chemical agents from people, equipment, and the environment to prevent further exposure and spread. Decontamination procedures must be carried out swiftly and efficiently to minimize the risk of secondary contamination. Law enforcement agencies also play a crucial role in the response, as they are responsible for securing the incident site, preserving evidence, and conducting investigations to determine the source and perpetrators of the attack.

In the longer term, the response to a chemical attack must also include efforts to recover and rebuild. This involves providing ongoing medical care and support to those affected by the attack, as well as addressing any psychological trauma that may have resulted. Additionally, efforts must be made to restore public confidence and return to normalcy as quickly as possible. This may involve repairing damaged infrastructure, providing financial assistance to affected individuals and businesses, and implementing measures to prevent future attacks.

Counterterrorism measures against chemical terrorism must also address the challenge of detecting and interdicting chemical weapons before they can be used. This involves the development and deployment of advanced detection technologies that can identify chemical agents in various environments. These technologies include portable detectors that can be used by first responders, as well as fixed sensors that can be installed in public spaces and critical infrastructure. The development of such technologies requires ongoing research and investment to keep pace with the evolving threat landscape.

International cooperation is another crucial element of counterterrorism measures against chemical terrorism. Terrorist organizations operate across borders, and the threat of chemical terrorism is a global concern. Therefore, it is essential for countries to work together to share intelligence, coordinate responses, and support each other's efforts to prevent and respond to chemical attacks. This cooperation can take the form of bilateral agreements between individual countries, as well as multilateral initiatives through international organizations such as the United Nations.

combating the financing of chemical terrorism is a critical component of counterterrorism efforts. Terrorist organizations require funding to acquire the materials and expertise necessary to carry out chemical attacks. Therefore, it is important to implement measures to disrupt the financial networks that support these activities. This includes monitoring financial transactions, freezing assets linked to terrorist organizations, and imposing sanctions on individuals and entities involved in the financing of chemical terrorism.

In addition to these measures, it is important to address the underlying factors that contribute to the threat of chemical terrorism. This includes addressing the root causes of terrorism, such as political instability, social inequality, and lack of economic opportunities. Efforts to promote peace, development, and human rights can help to reduce the appeal of terrorist ideologies and diminish the pool of individuals who might be recruited into terrorist organizations. Effective counterterrorism requires robust intelligence gathering, control of precursor chemicals, protection of critical infrastructure, healthcare preparedness, public awareness, rapid response capabilities, advanced detection technologies, international cooperation, and efforts to address the root causes of terrorism. By implementing these measures, societies can better protect themselves against the devastating effects of chemical terrorism and ensure a safer and more secure future.

Chapter 14: Terrorism and the Explosive Threat

The potential for terrorist groups to acquire explosives

One primary avenue through which terrorist groups acquire explosives is the legal market. Many countries have industries that utilize explosive materials for legitimate purposes, such as mining, construction, and demolition. The regulatory frameworks governing the sale and distribution of these materials vary significantly across regions, creating opportunities for exploitation. Terrorists may infiltrate these industries, posing as legitimate buyers, or corrupt insiders may facilitate the diversion of explosives to illicit networks. The relative ease of access to explosive materials in some regions underscores the need for stringent regulations and robust oversight to prevent their misuse.

The theft of explosives is another critical concern. Storage facilities, transportation routes, and even construction sites can become targets for terrorists seeking to acquire explosive materials. The lack of adequate security measures at these locations can lead to significant breaches, with potentially catastrophic consequences. Terrorist organizations often conduct meticulous planning and surveillance to identify vulnerabilities in the supply chain, exploiting weaknesses to their advantage. Enhanced security protocols, improved surveillance, and continuous monitoring are essential to mitigate the risk of theft and ensure the integrity of explosive supply chains.

Illicit manufacturing of explosives is a growing trend among terrorist groups. The knowledge required to produce improvised explosive devices (IEDs) is widely available, often disseminated through online platforms and dark web forums. This accessibility democratizes the capability to create deadly weapons, posing a significant threat. The materials needed for IEDs, such as fertilizers, chemicals, and household items, are often readily available and difficult to regulate effectively. Terrorist organizations leverage this accessibility to produce explosives in makeshift laboratories, circumventing traditional supply chains and law enforcement measures.

International smuggling networks play a crucial role in facilitating the acquisition of explosives by terrorist groups. These networks operate across borders, exploiting weak governance, corruption, and porous boundaries to transport explosive materials. The global nature of these networks makes them particularly challenging to dismantle, requiring coordinated international efforts and intelligence sharing. Terrorist groups often establish connections with organized crime syndicates, leveraging their expertise in smuggling and illicit trade to acquire explosives. Addressing this issue necessitates a comprehensive approach that includes strengthening border security, enhancing international cooperation, and disrupting financial flows that support these networks.

The role of technology in the acquisition and use of explosives by terrorist groups cannot be understated. Advances in communication and information technology have enabled terrorist organizations to share knowledge, coordinate activities, and recruit members more effectively. The internet provides a platform for the dissemination of bomb-making instructions, radicalization, and the mobilization of sympathizers. Encryption tools and anonymous online forums further complicate efforts to monitor and counter these activities. Law enforcement agencies must adapt to these technological challenges, developing sophisticated cyber capabilities to track and disrupt terrorist activities online.

The psychological and strategic motivations behind the use of explosives by terrorist groups are also significant. Explosives are chosen for their ability to create mass casualties, cause widespread destruction, and generate intense media coverage. The psychological impact of bombings can be profound, instilling fear, disrupting daily life, and undermining public confidence in security measures. Terrorist groups often seek to amplify this impact through strategic targeting, selecting high-profile locations, and timing attacks to maximize exposure. Understanding these motivations is crucial for developing effective counterterrorism strategies that address both the operational and ideological dimensions of terrorist activities.

The acquisition of explosives by terrorist groups is often intertwined with broader geopolitical and socio-economic factors. In regions experiencing conflict, instability, or weak governance, the barriers to acquiring explosives are significantly lower. Terrorist groups exploit these conditions to establish strongholds, recruit members, and access resources. The proliferation of armed groups, illicit trade, and corruption further exacerbates the challenge. Addressing the root causes of instability and strengthening governance structures are essential components of a long-term strategy to prevent the acquisition and use of explosives by terrorist groups.

Efforts to prevent terrorist groups from acquiring explosives must also consider the role of international cooperation and intelligence sharing. Terrorism is a transnational threat that requires a coordinated response. Information sharing between countries, intelligence agencies, and law enforcement bodies is crucial for identifying and disrupting terrorist networks. Collaborative initiatives, such as the Global Counterterrorism Forum and the United Nations Counter-Terrorism Committee, play a vital role in facilitating this cooperation. Strengthening these partnerships and enhancing the capacity of national and international institutions is essential for addressing the global challenge of terrorist acquisition of explosives.

Technological advancements also offer opportunities for improving the detection and prevention of explosive acquisition by terrorist groups. Innovations in surveillance technology, explosive detection systems, and data analytics can enhance the ability to identify and intercept illicit activities. The development of advanced screening technologies, such as trace detection and biometric identification, can improve security at critical infrastructure points and border crossings. Investing in research and development to stay ahead of emerging threats and leveraging technology to enhance situational awareness are critical components of a proactive counterterrorism strategy.

The legal and regulatory frameworks governing the control of explosive materials must be continuously reviewed and strengthened. International conventions, such as the Convention on the Marking of Plastic Explosives for the Purpose of Detection, provide a foundation for global efforts to regulate explosive materials. However, these frameworks must be complemented by robust national laws and enforcement mechanisms. Regular audits, inspections, and compliance checks are necessary to ensure that these laws are effectively implemented. Additionally, public awareness campaigns and community engagement can play a role in preventing the diversion of explosives to terrorist groups.

The role of intelligence agencies in preventing the acquisition of explosives by terrorist groups is paramount. Intelligence gathering and analysis provide the foundation for identifying threats, understanding terrorist networks, and preempting attacks. Human intelligence, signals intelligence, and open-source intelligence must be integrated to provide a comprehensive understanding of terrorist activities. The collaboration between intelligence agencies and law enforcement is essential for translating intelligence into actionable measures that prevent the acquisition and use of explosives by terrorist groups.

The threat posed by terrorist groups acquiring explosives is a dynamic and evolving challenge that requires a multifaceted and adaptive response. Addressing this issue involves a combination of stringent regulations, robust security measures, international cooperation, technological innovation, and strategic intelligence efforts. By understanding the various avenues through which terrorist groups acquire explosives and the motivations behind their use, policymakers and security professionals can develop more effective strategies to mitigate this threat and enhance global security. The continuous evolution of terrorist tactics and the shifting geopolitical landscape necessitate a proactive and flexible approach to counterterrorism, ensuring that efforts to prevent the acquisition of explosives remain relevant and effective in the face of emerging threats.

The consequences of an explosive terrorist attack

Beyond the immediate physical destruction, the psychological impact on survivors, first responders, and the broader community is profound. The trauma of witnessing or experiencing such violence can lead to long-term mental health issues, including post-traumatic stress disorder (PTSD), anxiety, depression, and a pervasive sense of insecurity. For first responders, the stress of handling such catastrophic events can result in burnout and secondary traumatization, necessitating targeted mental health support and counseling services. The broader community may experience heightened fear and anxiety, altering daily behaviors and routines as individuals and families adapt to a heightened threat environment.

The economic consequences of an explosive terrorist attack are substantial. The immediate costs include emergency response, medical care for the injured, and the extensive process of clearing and rebuilding the affected area. In the longer term, there are often significant declines in business activity and tourism, as both local residents and visitors avoid the area due to safety concerns. The disruption to commerce can have cascading effects on the local and national economy, leading to job losses and reduced economic growth. Additionally, the costs associated with increased security measures and the implementation of counterterrorism strategies place a further financial burden on governments and private sector entities.

Sociopolitically, the aftermath of a terrorist attack often leads to significant changes in public policy and law enforcement practices. Governments may implement stricter security measures, including enhanced surveillance, increased police presence, and more rigorous screening procedures at public eventos and transportation hubs. These measures, while aimed at preventing future attacks, can also raise concerns about civil liberties and the balance between security and individual freedoms. Public discourse often shifts towards issues of national security, immigration, and the role of government in protecting its citizens, sometimes leading to increased social and political polarization.

The media plays a critical role in shaping public perception and understanding of terrorist attacks. The immediate coverage of an explosive attack tends to be intense and pervasive, with around-the-clock reporting that can amplify the sense of fear and uncertainty. The way in which the media frames the event—whether emphasizing the heroism of first responders, the resilience of the community, or the threat posed by terrorism—can influence public attitudes and policy responses. Responsible journalism that provides accurate information and context is essential in helping the public navigate the complex emotional and practical challenges posed by such events.

In the international arena, a significant terrorist attack can lead to increased cooperation among nations in the fight against terrorism. Countries may share intelligence, coordinate border security measures, and collaborate on counterterrorism strategies. However, such cooperation can also lead to tensions, particularly if there are disagreements over the best approaches to counterterrorism or if certain nations are perceived as not doing enough to address the threat. The global nature of modern terrorism means that attacks in one part of the world can have ripple effects across borders, influencing international relations and security policies.

The response of the affected community is a critical factor in the recovery process. Community resilience—the ability to come together, support one another, and rebuild—plays a vital role in mitigating the long-term impacts of a terrorist attack. Grassroots initiatives, including support groups, memorial events, and community-led rebuilding efforts, can foster a sense of solidarity and help individuals and families cope with the trauma. Government and non-governmental organizations often play key roles in supporting these community-based efforts, providing resources, expertise, and coordination to aid in the recovery process.

The psychological and emotional recovery of individuals affected by a terrorist attack is a long-term process. Mental health professionals emphasize the importance of providing ongoing support and counseling to help individuals cope with trauma. This support must be culturally sensitive and tailored to the needs of different populations, recognizing that people experience and process trauma in diverse ways. Schools, workplaces, and community organizations can all play roles in providing support and creating environments that promote healing and resilience.

For policymakers and security professionals, the challenge is to balance the need for enhanced security with the protection of civil liberties. This requires a nuanced approach that considers the potential impacts of security measures on individual rights and freedoms. Transparent and accountable governance is essential in building public trust and ensuring that security measures are both effective and respectful of democratic values. Engaging with civil society organizations, human rights groups, and the broader public in the development of counterterrorism strategies can help achieve this balance.

The role of technology in both preventing and responding to terrorist attacks is increasingly significant. Advances in surveillance technology, data analytics, and communication systems can enhance the ability of law enforcement and security agencies to detect and prevent attacks. However, these technologies also raise ethical and privacy concerns that must be carefully managed. The use of artificial intelligence and machine learning in identifying potential threats, for example, must be balanced against the risk of bias and the need for human oversight to ensure fair and just outcomes.

In the educational sector, there is a growing emphasis on preparing professionals to deal with the complexities of terrorism and its aftermath. Academic programs in fields such as criminal justice, emergency management, and homeland security are increasingly incorporating coursework on terrorism, its psychological impacts, and effective response strategies. This educational focus helps ensure that future leaders and practitioners are well-equipped to address the multifaceted challenges posed by terrorism.

The role of international law and global cooperation in combating terrorism cannot be overstated. Agreements and conventions aimed at preventing the proliferation of weapons, including explosives, play a crucial role in reducing the threat of attacks. International bodies such as the United Nations work to foster collaboration among nations, promoting best practices in counterterrorism and supporting countries in building their capacity to prevent and respond to attacks. The immediate physical destruction and loss of life are accompanied by long-term psychological, economic, and sociopolitical impacts. The response to such attacks requires a comprehensive and coordinated effort, involving emergency services, mental health professionals, policymakers, educators, and the global community. By understanding the multifaceted nature of these consequences, societies can better prepare for and respond to the threat of terrorism, fostering resilience and ensuring the safety and well-being of their citizens.

The counterterrorism measures against explosive terrorism

Another pivotal aspect of counterterrorism measures is the enhancement of border security and customs controls. Strengthening these areas helps in intercepting the flow of explosives and precursor chemicals that could be used in the manufacture of IEDs. Advanced screening technologies, such as X-ray and tomography scanners, are employed at ports of entry to detect concealed explosives. Additionally, stringent regulations and monitoring of the sale and distribution of chemicals commonly used in bomb-making are crucial in preventing terrorists from acquiring the necessary materials.

Technological advancements play a significant role in countering explosive terrorism. The development and deployment of sophisticated detection systems, such as explosive trace detectors (ETDs) and vapor wake detection systems, have significantly improved the ability to detect explosive substances in various environments. These technologies are integrated into security protocols at airports, train stations, and other critical infrastructure points. Furthermore, the use of unmanned aerial vehicles (UAVs) and robotic systems for bomb detection and disposal has minimized the risk to human life during operations against

156

suspected explosive threats.

Training and preparedness are also essential components of counterterrorism strategies. Law enforcement and security personnel undergo rigorous training programs to recognize and respond to explosive threats effectively. This training includes the use of simulation exercises and scenario-based drills that replicate real-life situations. Such preparedness ensures that responders are well-equipped to handle explosive incidents swiftly and efficiently, thereby reducing casualties and minimizing damage.

Public awareness and community engagement are vital in countering the threat of explosive terrorism. Educating the public about the signs of suspicious activities and encouraging them to report any unusual behavior can serve as an additional layer of security. Community engagement programs foster trust between law enforcement agencies and the public, facilitating better cooperation and information sharing. This collaborative approach can lead to the early identification of potential threats and enhance overall security.

Legal frameworks and international cooperation are crucial in the fight against explosive terrorism. Comprehensive legal frameworks that criminalize the use, manufacture, and distribution of explosives for terrorist purposes provide the necessary legal basis for prosecuting offenders. International cooperation is equally important, as terrorist networks often operate across borders. Collaborative efforts among nations, such as joint intelligence operations, extradition treaties, and mutual legal assistance agreements, are essential in dismantling transnational terrorist networks and preventing the proliferation of explosive materials.

the role of cybersecurity in counterterrorism cannot be overlooked. Cyber tools and techniques are increasingly being used by terrorist organizations to coordinate attacks, disseminate propaganda, and recruit members. Counterterrorism agencies must therefore develop robust cyber capabilities to monitor and disrupt these online activities. This includes tracking communications on the dark web, identifying and neutralizing online radicalization efforts, and protecting critical infrastructure from cyber-attacks that could facilitate explosive terrorism.

In addition to proactive measures, reactive strategies are also integral to counterterrorism efforts. Rapid response teams, including bomb disposal units and specialized counterterrorism squads, are crucial in managing and mitigating the impact of explosive incidents. These teams are equipped with advanced tools and technologies to safely disarm or detonate explosive devices, thereby preventing or minimizing casualties. Post-incident analysis and debriefing are also essential to understand the modus operandi of terrorist groups and improve future response strategies.

The psychological dimension of counterterrorism is another critical area that warrants attention. Understanding the psychological profiles of terrorists and their motivations can inform more effective counterterrorism strategies. Psychological profiling and behavioral analysis can help in identifying potential terrorists before they commit acts of violence. Additionally, counter-radicalization programs aimed at addressing the root causes of radicalization and extremism can play a significant role in preventing the emergence of new terrorists.

To recapitulate, policy-making and legislative measures form the backbone of any counterterrorism strategy. Policymakers must continually review and update laws and regulations to address emerging threats and vulnerabilities. This includes enacting laws that enhance surveillance capabilities, strengthen penalties for terrorist-related offenses, and improve the coordination among various government agencies involved in counterterrorism efforts. Legislative measures should also ensure that the rights and freedoms of individuals are balanced with the need for security, thereby maintaining public trust and support for counterterrorism initiatives. By addressing the multifaceted nature of the threat, counterterrorism agencies can enhance their ability to prevent, detect, and respond to explosive terrorism effectively, thereby safeguarding public safety and national security.

Chapter 15:
Terrorism and the
Cyber Threat

The potential for terrorist groups to use cyber attacks

One of the primary reasons cyber attacks have become attractive to terrorist groups is the relative anonymity and low risk associated with conducting such operations. Unlike traditional forms of terrorism, which often involve physical presence and carry significant personal risk, cyber attacks can be orchestrated remotely, reducing the chances of detection and capture. This anonymity allows terrorist groups to execute attacks without the immediate threat of retaliation, enabling them to maintain operational security more effectively. The use of proxies and compromised systems further obscures the origins of the attack, making attribution challenging for law enforcement and intelligence agencies. This layer of deniability complicates the response mechanisms and can delay countermeasures, allowing terrorist groups to achieve their objectives with minimal interference.

the scalability and reach of cyber attacks provide terrorist groups with unprecedented capabilities. Traditional terrorist activities are often constrained by geographical and logistical limitations. In contrast, cyber attacks can be launched against targets anywhere in the world, transcending physical boundaries. This global reach allows terrorist groups to target critical infrastructure, financial systems, and governmental institutions with ease. The ability to disrupt essential services, such as power grids, water supply networks, and communication systems, can have far-reaching consequences, affecting not only the targeted country but also its allies and global stability. The potential to cause widespread chaos and economic damage makes cyber attacks a potent tool for terrorist groups aiming to achieve their strategic goals.

The financial aspect of cyber attacks also plays a crucial role in their appeal to terrorist groups. Traditional forms of terrorism, such as bombings or physical assaults, require considerable resources, including funding, logistics, and personnel. Cyber attacks, on the other hand, can be executed at a fraction of the cost. The proliferation of hacking tools and the availability of exploit kits on the dark web have lowered the barrier to entry, allowing even relatively small and less well-funded groups to launch sophisticated cyber attacks. This cost-effectiveness enables terrorist groups to allocate their resources more efficiently, potentially increasing the frequency and scale of their operations. Additionally, cyber attacks can generate revenue for terrorist organizations through methods such as ransomware, enabling them to fund further activities and sustain their operations over the long term.

The psychological impact of cyber attacks is another critical factor that enhances their attractiveness to terrorist groups. Traditional acts of terrorism, while devastating, often have a limited psychological impact beyond the immediate victims and their families. Cyber attacks, however, can create a pervasive sense of fear and uncertainty on a much larger scale. The disruption of essential services, the loss of personal data, and the exposure of sensitive information can undermine public trust in institutions and create widespread panic. The psychological warfare aspect of cyber attacks can be just as damaging, if not more so, than the physical destruction caused by traditional terrorist activities. The constant threat of cyber attacks can lead to heightened anxiety and a sense of vulnerability among the population, which can be exploited by terrorist groups to further their ideological agendas.

The strategic objectives of terrorist groups can also be effectively advanced through cyber attacks. Many terrorist organizations seek to undermine the stability and legitimacy of governments, and cyber attacks offer a means to achieve this goal.

By targeting critical infrastructure and governmental institutions, terrorist groups can disrupt the functioning of the state, eroding public confidence in its ability to protect its citizens. The economic impact of cyber attacks can further weaken the target country, potentially leading to political instability and social unrest. In regions where terrorist groups are seeking to establish a foothold or expand their influence, cyber attacks can serve as a powerful tool to destabilize the existing order and create opportunities for the group to assert control.

Furthermore, cyber attacks can be used to amplify the impact of traditional forms of terrorism. For instance, a cyber attack can be coordinated with a physical attack to maximize confusion and hinder the response efforts. Disrupting communication networks during a terrorist incident can impede the coordination of emergency services, exacerbating the consequences of the attack. Similarly, cyber attacks can be used to spread propaganda and misinformation, furthering the narrative of the terrorist group and increasing their visibility. The ability to manipulate information and control the narrative in the aftermath of an attack can significantly enhance the psychological and strategic impact of terrorist activities.

The evolving nature of cyber threats also presents challenges for counterterrorism efforts. Traditional methods of counterterrorism, such as surveillance and intelligence gathering, are often less effective in the cyber domain. Terrorist groups can exploit the anonymity and decentralized nature of the internet to evade detection and circumvent security measures. The rapid pace of technological advancements means that new vulnerabilities and attack vectors are constantly emerging, making it difficult for authorities to stay ahead of the threat. The need for continuous innovation and adaptation in cyber defense strategies is paramount to effectively counter the evolving tactics of terrorist groups.

the international dimension of cyber attacks adds another layer of complexity to counterterrorism efforts. The borderless nature of the internet means that cyber attacks can originate from anywhere in the world, complicating attribution and response efforts. International cooperation and information sharing are crucial in addressing this challenge, but differences in legal frameworks, jurisdictional issues, and political considerations can hinder effective collaboration. The need for a coordinated global response to cyber threats is essential to mitigate the risks posed by terrorist groups and ensure a unified and effective approach to counterterrorism in the digital age.

In addition to the operational and strategic advantages, the potential for cyber attacks to serve as a tool for recruitment and radicalization cannot be overlooked. The internet provides a platform for terrorist groups to disseminate their ideology, recruit new members, and coordinate activities. Cyber attacks can be used to draw attention to the group's cause, attract sympathizers, and radicalize individuals who may be inspired by the perceived success and impact of such attacks. The online presence of terrorist groups allows them to reach a global audience, spreading their message and gaining support from individuals who may feel marginalized or disillusioned with mainstream society. The ability to recruit and radicalize individuals through cyber means enhances the long-term sustainability and reach of terrorist groups, posing a significant challenge to counterterrorism efforts.

The intersection of cyber attacks and terrorism also raises important ethical and legal considerations. The use of offensive cyber operations by states to preemptively target terrorist groups or disrupt their activities raises questions about proportionality, collateral damage, and the potential for escalation. The legal framework governing cyber operations is still evolving, and there is a need for clear guidelines and international agreements to regulate the use of cyber capabilities in counterterrorism. Balancing the need for security with respect for human rights and the rule of law is a critical challenge that policymakers and legal experts must address to ensure that counterterrorism efforts remain effective and ethical. The anonymity, scalability, and low cost of cyber attacks make them an attractive tool for terrorist groups seeking to achieve their strategic objectives. The psychological impact, strategic advantages, and potential for recruitment and radicalization further underscore the importance of addressing this threat. Effective counterterrorism strategies must encompass robust cyber defenses, international cooperation, and a commitment to ethical and legal principles. By understanding the motivations and capabilities of terrorist groups in the cyber domain, policymakers and security professionals can develop more effective and resilient approaches to countering this complex and dynamic threat.

The consequences of a cyber terrorist attack

One of the most immediate and tangible consequences of a cyber terrorist attack is economic disruption. Modern economies are heavily reliant on digital infrastructure for financial transactions, trade, communication, and the provision of essential services. A successful cyber terrorist attack on critical infrastructure, such as banking systems, stock exchanges, or utilities, can lead to significant economic losses. For instance, an attack that disables online banking services or disrupts electronic payment systems can impede economic activities, leading to financial instability and loss of consumer confidence. the costs associated with responding to and recovering from such attacks can be astronomical. Businesses may incur expenses related to system repairs, data recovery, and enhanced cybersecurity measures, while governments may need to allocate substantial resources to mitigate the effects and bolster national cybersecurity defenses.

Beyond economic impacts, cyber terrorist attacks can have profound social consequences. In an interconnected world where digital communication is integral to daily life, disruptions to communication networks can isolate individuals and communities, creating panic and uncertainty. For example, an attack that compromises emergency communication systems can hinder the ability of first responders to address crises effectively, exacerbating the impact of natural disasters or other emergencies. Additionally, cyber attacks that target social media platforms or news outlets can spread misinformation and propaganda, undermining public trust in information sources and destabilizing social cohesion. The psychological effects of such attacks can be significant, leading to heightened anxiety, fear, and a sense of vulnerability among the populace.

The psychological dimension of cyber terrorism is particularly insidious. Unlike physical acts of terrorism, which often produce visible and immediate harm, cyber attacks can be covert and insidious, creating a sense of unease and paranoia. The anonymity and remoteness of cyber terrorists allow them to operate with relative impunity, making it challenging for authorities to identify and apprehend perpetrators. This lack of accountability can amplify the psychological impact on victims, who may feel powerless and uncertain about their safety. Furthermore, the constant threat of cyber attacks can erode public trust in digital technologies, leading to a reluctance to adopt new technologies or engage in online activities. This can stifle innovation and hinder the development of digital economies, ultimately affecting societal progress.

Politically, cyber terrorist attacks can have far-reaching implications for national security and international relations. Governments worldwide are increasingly recognizing the strategic importance of cybersecurity and the need to protect critical infrastructure from cyber threats. A successful cyber terrorist attack can undermine national security by compromising sensitive government data, disrupting military operations, or interfering with electoral processes. The potential for cyber attacks to influence political outcomes or sow discord among populations poses a significant threat to democratic institutions and governance. the borderless nature of cyber space means that cyber terrorist attacks can have international ramifications, potentially leading to conflicts between states. Attribution of cyber attacks is notoriously difficult, and the risk of misattribution or false flag operations can escalate tensions and lead to geopolitical instability.

The strategic objectives of cyber terrorists often align with those of traditional terrorists, including the desire to instill fear, disrupt societal norms, and achieve political or ideological goals. However, the methods and tools employed in cyber terrorism differ significantly from those used in conventional terrorism. Cyber terrorists leverage sophisticated hacking techniques, malware, and other cyber tools to achieve their objectives, often exploiting vulnerabilities in software and hardware to gain unauthorized access to systems. The decentralized and global nature of the internet allows cyber terrorists to operate across borders, making it challenging for any single nation to combat this threat unilaterally. International cooperation and coordination are essential to effectively address the threat of cyber terrorism, requiring collaboration between governments, private sector entities, and international organizations.

The role of non-state actors in cyber terrorism is also a significant concern. While state-sponsored cyber attacks are a recognized threat, non-state actors, including terrorist groups, criminal organizations, and hacktivist collectives, have increasingly demonstrated the capability and intent to conduct cyber attacks. These actors often operate with different motivations and objectives, ranging from financial gain to political activism. The convergence of cyber capabilities with traditional terrorist tactics can create hybrid threats that are difficult to predict and counter. For example, a terrorist group might use cyber attacks to disable security systems, enabling a physical attack on a critical infrastructure target. The potential for such synergistic threats underscores the need for a comprehensive and integrated approach to cybersecurity that addresses both cyber and physical dimensions of terrorism.

The challenge of attribution in cyber terrorism further complicates the response to these threats. Unlike traditional terrorism, where the perpetrators can often be identified through physical evidence and intelligence, cyber attacks can be launched from anywhere in the world, obscuring the identity and location of the attackers. This anonymity can embolden cyber terrorists, allowing them to carry out attacks with relative impunity. The difficulty of attribution also poses challenges for international law and enforcement, as it complicates efforts to hold perpetrators accountable and deter future attacks. Developing robust mechanisms for cyber attribution, including advanced forensic techniques and international legal frameworks, is crucial to strengthening global cybersecurity and deterring cyber terrorism.

Efforts to mitigate the consequences of cyber terrorist attacks must also focus on enhancing resilience and preparedness. This includes investing in cybersecurity infrastructure, developing robust incident response capabilities, and fostering a culture of cybersecurity awareness among individuals and organizations. Public-private partnerships are essential to leverage the expertise and resources of both sectors in addressing cyber threats.

Additionally, international cooperation is vital to share information, best practices, and intelligence on cyber threats, enabling a coordinated response to cyber terrorism. The establishment of international norms and agreements on cybersecurity can help create a framework for collective action against cyber terrorism, promoting stability and security in the digital age. The increasing reliance on digital infrastructure in modern society makes the threat of cyber terrorism particularly acute, requiring a comprehensive and collaborative approach to cybersecurity. Addressing the threat of cyber terrorism necessitates not only technological solutions but also strategic initiatives to build resilience, enhance preparedness, and foster international cooperation. By understanding the complex and interconnected nature of cyber threats, governments, organizations, and individuals can better protect themselves against the potentially devastating consequences of cyber terrorist attacks.

The counterterrorism measures against cyber terrorism

One of the primary counterterrorism measures against cyber terrorism is the enhancement of cybersecurity infrastructure. This includes the development and implementation of robust security protocols, regular updates to software and hardware, and the establishment of dedicated cybersecurity units within governmental and private sector organizations. These measures are designed to prevent cyber attacks by identifying and addressing vulnerabilities before they can be exploited by terrorists. The focus on cybersecurity infrastructure is crucial because it serves as the first line of defense against cyber terrorism, ensuring that critical systems remain secure and operational.

In addition to enhancing cybersecurity infrastructure, counterterrorism efforts also involve proactive intelligence gathering and analysis. This aspect of counterterrorism is essential for identifying potential threats and understanding the strategies and motivations of cyber terrorists. Intelligence agencies use a variety of methods to gather information, including monitoring online activities, analyzing communication networks, and collaborating with international partners. The goal is to detect and disrupt terrorist plots before they can be executed. This proactive approach requires a high level of expertise in both cyber technology and counterterrorism strategies, as well as the ability to adapt to the constantly changing tactics of cyber terrorists.

Another critical component of counterterrorism measures against cyber terrorism is the development of international cooperation and collaboration. Cyber threats do not recognize national borders, and effective counterterrorism efforts require a coordinated response from multiple countries. This includes sharing intelligence, coordinating responses to cyber attacks, and developing joint strategies to prevent future incidents. International cooperation is also important for establishing legal frameworks and agreements that facilitate the prosecution of cyber terrorists. By working together, countries can create a more comprehensive and effective defense against cyber terrorism.

The psychological dimension of counterterrorism measures against cyber terrorism involves understanding the motivations and behaviors of cyber terrorists. This understanding is crucial for developing strategies that can effectively counter the psychological aspects of cyber terrorism. Cyber terrorists often seek to exploit fear and uncertainty, and counterterrorism efforts must address these psychological tactics. This can involve public awareness campaigns that educate the public about the nature of cyber threats and how to protect themselves. It can also involve efforts to counter the propaganda and recruitment efforts of terrorist groups online. By addressing the psychological aspects of cyber terrorism, counterterrorism measures can reduce the impact of these attacks and prevent the spread of fear and panic.

Education and training are also essential components of counterterrorism measures against cyber terrorism. This includes training for cybersecurity professionals, law enforcement agencies, and the general public. Cybersecurity professionals need to be equipped with the latest knowledge and skills to effectively protect against cyber threats. Law enforcement agencies require specialized training to investigate and respond to cyber attacks. The general public also needs to be educated about the risks of cyber terrorism and how to recognize and respond to potential threats. By investing in education and training, counterterrorism efforts can build a more resilient and informed society that is better prepared to face the challenges of cyber terrorism.

The legal and regulatory framework for counterterrorism measures against cyber terrorism is another important aspect. This includes laws and regulations that govern the use of digital technologies, as well as the prosecution of cyber terrorists. Legal frameworks need to be updated regularly to keep pace with the rapidly evolving nature of cyber threats. They also need to strike a balance between protecting national security and safeguarding individual privacy and civil liberties. Effective legal and regulatory frameworks can provide a strong foundation for counterterrorism efforts, ensuring that they are conducted within a clear and consistent legal framework.

The role of technology in counterterrorism measures against cyber terrorism cannot be overstated. Advanced technologies such as artificial intelligence, machine learning, and big data analytics are increasingly being used to detect and prevent cyber attacks. These technologies can analyze vast amounts of data to identify patterns and anomalies that may indicate a cyber threat. They can also automate responses to cyber attacks, allowing for faster and more effective countermeasures. The use of advanced technologies in counterterrorism efforts is a critical factor in staying ahead of cyber terrorists and protecting against future attacks.

Public-private partnerships are also an essential element of counterterrorism measures against cyber terrorism. These partnerships involve collaboration between government agencies and private sector organizations to share information, resources, and expertise. Public-private partnerships can enhance the overall effectiveness of counterterrorism efforts by leveraging the strengths of both sectors. For example, private sector organizations often have access to cutting-edge technologies and expertise that can be valuable in countering cyber threats. Government agencies, on the other hand, have the authority and resources to coordinate and implement large-scale counterterrorism strategies. By working together, public and private sector organizations can create a more comprehensive and effective defense against cyber terrorism.

The threat of cyber terrorism also highlights the importance of resilience and recovery planning. Counterterrorism measures need to include strategies for responding to and recovering from cyber attacks. This involves developing contingency plans, conducting regular drills and exercises, and establishing mechanisms for quickly restoring critical systems and services. Resilience and recovery planning are essential for minimizing the impact of cyber attacks and ensuring that societies can quickly return to normalcy after an incident. Effective resilience and recovery planning can also deter cyber terrorists by demonstrating that their attacks will not achieve the desired impact.

The ethical considerations of counterterrorism measures against cyber terrorism are also a critical concern. Counterterrorism efforts must be conducted in a manner that respects human rights and civil liberties. This includes ensuring that surveillance and intelligence-gathering activities are conducted within a legal and ethical framework. It also involves addressing the potential for bias and discrimination in counterterrorism measures. Ethical considerations are important for maintaining public trust and support for counterterrorism efforts. They also help to ensure that counterterrorism measures are effective and sustainable in the long term.

The threat of cyber terrorism is constantly evolving, and counterterrorism measures must be adaptable and flexible to keep pace with these changes. This requires ongoing research and development to stay ahead of emerging threats. It also involves continuously evaluating and updating counterterrorism strategies to ensure that they remain effective. The dynamic nature of cyber terrorism means that counterterrorism efforts must be proactive and forward-looking, anticipating future threats and developing strategies to address them. By staying ahead of the curve, counterterrorism measures can effectively protect against the evolving threat of cyber terrorism. This approach includes enhancing cybersecurity infrastructure, proactive intelligence gathering, international cooperation, addressing psychological aspects, education and training, legal and regulatory frameworks, advanced technologies, public-private partnerships, resilience and recovery planning, and ethical considerations. By addressing these various aspects, counterterrorism efforts can effectively protect against the threat of cyber terrorism and ensure the security and stability of societies in the digital age.

Chapter 16:
Terrorism and the
Humanitarian Crisis

The impact of terrorism on civilians

In the immediate aftermath of a terrorist attack, the psychological toll on civilians is evident in the heightened state of alertness and hypervigilance that many individuals adopt. This state of heightened awareness is a natural response to perceived threats, but it can also become maladaptive, leading to chronic stress and anxiety disorders. Civilians may experience flashbacks, nightmares, and intrusive thoughts related to the traumatic event, significantly impairing their daily functioning and quality of life. The mental health impacts can extend beyond the immediate victims to affect broader segments of the population, as the pervasive fear of future attacks spreads through communities.

The social consequences of terrorism are equally profound. Terrorism can erode social cohesion and trust within communities, as fear and suspicion become pervasive. The breakdown of trust can lead to the stigmatization and marginalization of certain groups, particularly if the terrorist acts are perpetrated by individuals or groups from specific ethnic, religious, or ideological backgrounds. This can exacerbate existing social divides and foster an environment of intolerance and discrimination. The social fabric of communities can be further strained by the increased presence of security measures and military interventions, which, while intended to enhance safety, can also contribute to a sense of occupation and oppression.

Economically, terrorism inflicts significant damage on civilians and their livelihoods. The immediate aftermath of an attack often results in loss of life, injury, and destruction of property, leading to direct economic costs. Beyond these immediate impacts, terrorism can disrupt economic activities and deter investment, tourism, and trade. The fear of future attacks can lead to reduced consumer confidence and spending, impacting local economies and exacerbating unemployment and poverty. In regions heavily reliant on tourism or foreign investment, the economic repercussions can be particularly severe, leading to long-term economic decline and increased hardship for civilians.

The educational sector is another area significantly affected by terrorism. Schools and universities can become targets of attacks, disrupting the education of children and young adults. The fear of attacks can lead to school closures and a decline in educational attainment, with long-term implications for the social and economic development of affected regions. The disruption of education can limit opportunities for future generations, perpetuating cycles of poverty and instability.

Healthcare systems also bear a heavy burden in the wake of terrorist attacks. The immediate response to an attack requires significant medical resources to treat the injured and manage the psychological trauma of survivors. Hospitals and healthcare facilities may become overwhelmed, and the long-term care needs of those affected by terrorism can strain healthcare systems, diverting resources from other critical areas. The psychological impact on healthcare workers, who often face secondary trauma from treating victims of terrorism, can also have significant consequences for the healthcare system's capacity to respond effectively to future crises.

The impact of terrorism on civilians is not uniform and can vary significantly depending on the context and nature of the attacks. In conflict zones, where terrorist acts are often part of broader insurgencies or civil wars, civilians may face compounded challenges, including displacement, loss of property, and ongoing threats to their safety. The presence of armed groups and the breakdown of law and order can create environments where civilians are subjected to multiple forms of violence and exploitation. In these contexts, the lines between terrorism and other forms of violence can become blurred, making it difficult to isolate the specific impacts of terrorism on civilians.

The strategies employed by terrorists to maximize the impact on civilians are often designed to exploit vulnerabilities and create a climate of fear. Terrorists frequently target symbolic locations, public spaces, and large gatherings to inflict maximum casualties and garner media attention. The use of indiscriminate violence against civilians is a hallmark of terrorist tactics, aimed at creating a sense of pervasive threat and undermining public confidence in the ability of authorities to provide security. The psychological impact of such attacks is amplified by media coverage, which can spread fear and anxiety far beyond the immediate vicinity of the attack.

The media plays a crucial role in shaping public perceptions of terrorism and its impact on civilians. While media coverage can raise awareness and mobilize support for affected communities, it can also contribute to sensationalism and the spread of fear. The 24-hour news cycle and the proliferation of social media platforms mean that images and reports of terrorist attacks can be disseminated rapidly and widely, magnifying the psychological impact on the public. The constant exposure to violent imagery and narratives of terrorism can lead to a phenomenon known as "mean world syndrome," where individuals perceive the world as more dangerous than it actually is, further heightening fear and anxiety.

Governments and international organizations face significant challenges in addressing the impact of terrorism on civilians. Effective counterterrorism strategies must balance the need for security with the protection of civil liberties and human rights. Overly aggressive or indiscriminate counterterrorism measures can exacerbate the social and psychological impacts on civilians, leading to resentment and further radicalization. A comprehensive approach to counterterrorism must include efforts to address the root causes of terrorism, such as political marginalization, economic inequality, and social exclusion. By promoting inclusive governance, economic development, and social cohesion, governments can help mitigate the conditions that give rise to terrorism and reduce its impact on civilians.

International cooperation is also essential in addressing the transnational nature of terrorism. Terrorist networks often operate across borders, exploiting weaknesses in national security systems and taking advantage of regional instability. Effective counterterrorism efforts require coordinated intelligence sharing, joint military operations, and collaborative efforts to disrupt terrorist financing and recruitment. International organizations, such as the United Nations, play a critical role in facilitating this cooperation and providing support to countries affected by terrorism. Humanitarian organizations also play a vital role in providing relief and support to civilians affected by terrorism, including medical care, psychological support, and assistance with displacement and recovery. The strategies employed by terrorists to maximize their impact on civilians underscore the need for comprehensive and multifaceted responses. Addressing the root causes of terrorism, promoting inclusive governance, and fostering international cooperation are essential components of an effective response. By understanding the complex and interrelated impacts of terrorism on civilians, policymakers and practitioners can develop more effective strategies to mitigate its effects and support affected communities in their recovery and resilience-building efforts.

The humanitarian assistance for victims of terrorism

The immediate medical response to a terrorist attack is crucial for saving lives and mitigating long-term physical damage. Emergency medical teams must be equipped to handle a high volume of casualties with varying degrees of injury. These teams often operate in chaotic and dangerous environments, requiring specialized training and equipment to ensure their safety and effectiveness. The provision of timely and appropriate medical care can significantly reduce mortality rates and improve the prognosis for survivors. medical interventions must be complemented by psychological support to address the trauma experienced by victims. This support is vital in preventing the development of chronic psychological conditions such as post-traumatic stress disorder

(PTSD), anxiety, and depression.

Beyond immediate medical and psychological support, victims of terrorism often require long-term economic assistance. Terrorist attacks can result in the loss of livelihoods, either through injury, death, or the destruction of property and businesses. Economic aid in the form of compensation, grants, and vocational training programs can help victims regain financial independence and stability. This assistance is particularly important in regions where terrorist activities have disrupted local economies and exacerbated poverty. By providing economic support, humanitarian organizations can help victims avoid the cycle of poverty and dependence that can result from terrorist violence.

Social reintegration is another critical aspect of humanitarian assistance for victims of terrorism. Individuals who have suffered severe injuries or psychological trauma may find it challenging to return to their previous roles within their communities. Programs aimed at social reintegration focus on helping victims rebuild their social networks, regain their sense of belonging, and participate fully in community life. These programs often involve collaboration with local community leaders, religious institutions, and social organizations to create a supportive environment for victims. Social reintegration efforts are essential for preventing the marginalization of victims and promoting social cohesion in the aftermath of a terrorist attack.

The role of international cooperation in humanitarian assistance cannot be overstated. Terrorism is a global issue that transcends national borders, necessitating a coordinated international response. International organizations, such as the United Nations and the International Committee of the Red Cross, play a pivotal role in coordinating and delivering humanitarian aid to victims of terrorism. These organizations leverage their global reach and expertise to ensure that aid is distributed efficiently and effectively. Additionally, international cooperation facilitates the sharing of best practices and resources, enhancing the overall quality and impact of humanitarian assistance.

Funding is a significant challenge in providing humanitarian assistance to victims of terrorism. The costs associated with emergency medical care, long-term rehabilitation, and economic support can be substantial. Governments, international organizations, and private donors must commit to sustained and adequate funding to ensure that humanitarian efforts are not hampered by financial constraints. transparency and accountability in the use of funds are essential to maintain public trust and ensure that resources are used effectively to benefit victims. Innovative funding mechanisms, such as public-private partnerships and crowdfunding, can also play a role in mobilizing resources for humanitarian assistance.

In addition to financial resources, the effectiveness of humanitarian assistance for victims of terrorism depends on the capacity and preparedness of aid organizations. Training and equipping aid workers to respond to terrorist attacks require ongoing investment in professional development and logistical support. Aid organizations must be prepared to operate in high-risk environments and adapt to rapidly changing circumstances. This preparedness includes having contingency plans for various scenarios, ensuring the availability of necessary supplies, and establishing communication networks to coordinate responses. The capacity-building efforts of aid organizations are critical in enhancing their ability to provide timely and effective assistance to victims.

The ethical considerations in providing humanitarian assistance to victims of terrorism are complex and multifaceted. Aid organizations must navigate issues such as neutrality, impartiality, and the protection of human rights. Maintaining neutrality is crucial in ensuring that aid is not perceived as being aligned with any particular political or ideological agenda. Impartiality requires that aid be distributed based on need, without discrimination. Protecting human rights involves ensuring that victims are treated with dignity and respect and that their fundamental rights are upheld. Ethical considerations also extend to the treatment of aid workers, who must be safeguarded against the risks associated with operating in conflict zones.

The psychological impact of terrorism on victims and aid workers is an area that requires particular attention. Victims of terrorism often experience severe psychological trauma, which can have long-

lasting effects on their mental health and well-being.
Psychological support services, including counseling, therapy, and
support groups, are essential in helping victims cope with their
experiences and rebuild their lives. Similarly, aid workers who are
exposed to traumatic events in the course of their work are at risk
of developing secondary trauma or burnout. Providing psychological
support and counseling to aid workers is crucial in maintaining
their mental health and ensuring their ability to continue
providing effective assistance.

The role of education and awareness in humanitarian assistance for
victims of terrorism is also significant. Educating communities
about the risks and impacts of terrorism can help prevent attacks
and mitigate their effects. Awareness campaigns can promote
resilience and preparedness, empowering communities to respond
effectively in the event of an attack. Additionally, education
programs can foster a culture of empathy and support for victims,
reducing stigma and promoting social inclusion. By raising
awareness and promoting education, humanitarian organizations can
enhance the overall effectiveness of their assistance efforts.
Addressing the immediate and long-term needs of victims, ensuring
adequate funding, maintaining ethical standards, and providing
psychological support are all essential components of effective
humanitarian assistance. By prioritizing the well-being of victims
and promoting social stability, humanitarian organizations play a
crucial role in mitigating the impact of terrorism and fostering
resilience in affected communities.

The prevention of future humanitarian crises

Understanding the psychological underpinnings of terrorism is
pivotal in devising effective preventive strategies. The
motivations behind terrorist acts are complex, often rooted in a
combination of ideological fervor, socio-economic grievances, and
political disenfranchisement. Addressing these underlying causes
requires a nuanced approach that encompasses both security and
developmental measures. Enhancing intelligence capabilities to
preempt terrorist activities is crucial, but equally important is
the investment in social and economic development to alleviate the

conditions that foster radicalization.

Education and awareness programs play a critical role in preventing the spread of extremist ideologies. By promoting critical thinking and tolerance, these programs can inoculate vulnerable populations against the seductive narratives of terrorist organizations. fostering intercultural and interfaith dialogue can bridge divides and reduce the appeal of extremist ideologies. In this regard, civil society organizations, educational institutions, and religious leaders have significant roles to play in building resilient communities that can withstand the pressures of radicalization.

Effective governance and the rule of law are fundamental in preventing humanitarian crises exacerbated by terrorism. Weak governance structures, corruption, and lack of accountability create environments in which terrorist groups can thrive. Strengthening institutions, ensuring transparent and accountable governance, and upholding the rule of law are essential components of a preventive strategy. This involves not only building the capacity of state institutions but also ensuring that they are responsive to the needs and aspirations of the populace.

Economic development and poverty alleviation are integral to preventing the conditions that give rise to terrorism and humanitarian crises. Poverty, unemployment, and lack of economic opportunities can drive individuals towards extremist groups that promise a better future. Therefore, comprehensive economic policies that promote inclusive growth, create jobs, and reduce poverty are vital. International development assistance should be directed towards building sustainable economies that can provide long-term stability and prosperity.

The role of international cooperation in preventing humanitarian crises related to terrorism cannot be overstated. Terrorism is a transnational threat that requires coordinated efforts across borders. Sharing intelligence, collaborating on law enforcement, and engaging in joint military operations are crucial in dismantling terrorist networks. Furthermore, international cooperation in addressing the root causes of terrorism, such as poverty, inequality, and lack of education, can significantly reduce the risk of future crises.

Humanitarian interventions must be designed with a long-term perspective to prevent the recurrence of crises. While immediate relief efforts are essential in mitigating the impacts of terrorism-related humanitarian crises, sustainable development initiatives are necessary to address the underlying issues. This involves rebuilding infrastructure, restoring essential services, and creating economic opportunities for affected populations. ensuring the protection of human rights and promoting social justice are critical in rebuilding trust and fostering resilience in post-crisis environments.

The media plays a significant role in shaping public perceptions of terrorism and humanitarian crises. Responsible and ethical reporting can help mitigate the sensationalism that often accompanies terrorist acts, reducing the fear and hysteria that terrorists aim to incite. By providing accurate and balanced information, the media can contribute to informed public discourse and support preventive measures. Additionally, the media can highlight positive stories of resilience and recovery, which can inspire hope and mobilize support for preventive actions.

Community-based approaches are crucial in preventing future humanitarian crises linked to terrorism. Local communities often have the best understanding of the dynamics and vulnerabilities within their areas. Empowering communities through participatory decision-making, providing resources for local initiatives, and supporting grassroots organizations can enhance their capacity to prevent radicalization and respond to crises. Community policing and local surveillance mechanisms can also be effective in identifying and addressing early signs of radicalization and violence.

Technology and innovation offer new tools for preventing humanitarian crises associated with terrorism. Advances in data analytics, artificial intelligence, and social media monitoring can enhance the ability to detect and disrupt terrorist activities. These technologies can also be used to monitor social trends and identify potential hotspots of radicalization. However, it is essential to balance the use of technology with respect for privacy and human rights to avoid creating new sources of tension and mistrust.

The role of women in preventing terrorism and humanitarian crises is often underappreciated. Women can be powerful agents of change in their communities, advocating for peace and reconciliation. Empowering women through education, economic opportunities, and political participation can strengthen community resilience and reduce the vulnerability to extremist ideologies. Women's involvement in peacebuilding and conflict resolution processes is also crucial in ensuring sustainable and inclusive solutions.

Addressing the psychological trauma caused by terrorism and humanitarian crises is essential for long-term prevention. Mental health support for affected individuals and communities can help mitigate the long-term impacts of violence and instability. Psychosocial programs that provide counseling, support groups, and trauma-informed care can aid in the recovery process and build resilience against future crises. Furthermore, integrating mental health services into broader development and humanitarian programs ensures that the psychological needs of affected populations are adequately addressed.

Environmental factors also play a role in the prevention of humanitarian crises linked to terrorism. Environmental degradation, climate change, and resource scarcity can exacerbate existing tensions and create conditions conducive to radicalization and violence. Sustainable environmental management, coupled with climate adaptation and mitigation strategies, can reduce these risks. Promoting environmental awareness and integrating environmental considerations into development planning can contribute to long-term stability and prevent crises.

The role of the international community in supporting national efforts to prevent humanitarian crises related to terrorism is vital. This includes providing financial and technical assistance, sharing best practices, and facilitating capacity-building initiatives. Multilateral institutions, such as the United Nations, can play a coordinating role in mobilizing international support and ensuring that preventive measures are comprehensive and coherent. Additionally, regional organizations can facilitate cooperation among neighboring countries to address cross-border threats and promote regional stability. By combining security measures with developmental initiatives, promoting education and dialogue, strengthening governance, and fostering international cooperation, it is possible to build resilient societies that can withstand the pressures of radicalization and violence. The involvement of local communities, the use of technology, the empowerment of women, and the provision of mental health support are all essential components of a comprehensive preventive strategy. Ultimately, a concerted and sustained effort by all stakeholders is necessary to create a safer and more stable world.

Printed in Dunstable, United Kingdom